White Powder Fences

By Ingrid O. Duva

&

Betty O. McAleer

CONTENTS

White Powder Fences

There was a knock on the door. Octavio had been waiting for a package to arrive. He opened the door and a stranger handed him a briefcase. Octavio walked into the kitchen and placed it on the table. He stared at the leather package with burning curiosity. Before he could open it, the phone rang. It was a call from Colombia.

"Hello."

"Hello Octavio. Did you get it?"

"Yes."

"Did you open it?"

"No."

"Go ahead, open it."

"Octavio, you see what's in it?"

"Yes."

"Ten percent is yours if you agree to bring it to Barranquilla."

"Ok, let me call you back."

"Hurry, I need a confirmation."

Octavio could barely contain his enthusiasm as he revealed his brother's proposition. Beatrice wanted no part of it but Octavio trusted his brother and did not think it was a big deal. He assured her it would be a short trip. "Beatrice, what are you afraid of? I don't want to lose my job. I'll be back in two days."

Beatrice remained silent as Octavio went on, "We really need the money! I have been working long hours and we are barely making it. Did you see that stack? There might be enough there for us to buy a house."

They had been living in the United States for five years. Octavio worked as a salesman for an American corporation, but he struggled financially so it was easy to allow the allure of money to cloud his perspective. Money was scarce but in this foreign place Beatrice had found the peace that she had never felt in her homeland. This new plan was destroying her hope to be rid of all her past troubles with Octavio. "Octavio, I don't want to risk what we've built here. This is our new home, the birthplace of our son, and Josefina seems very happy."

Octavio went on, "I want to take Gabriel. My family has never met him and I want to show off my handsome son."

Hearing these words were like a kick in her stomach. Her memories of Colombia were still raw. All the women, the disappearing acts with his brother, the sleepless nights, all of it stormed back in that moment. In a near whisper she responded, "I may not be a worldly woman but it seems obvious to me that traveling with a bag full of money from the United States to Colombia is very risky."

Octavio ignored her concerns and a minute later said, "My family has not met Gabriel yet and my mother is very old. I want her to see how handsome he is."

Beatrice stood quiet as she secretly prayed. She pondered the idea for a short while and finally arrived at the conclusion that Octavio always did what he wanted. It occurred to her that allowing Gabriel to go might not be a bad idea since it would certainly assure their prompt return. She reluctantly agreed and hoped this would not be a regrettable decision.

CHAPTER 1

Colombia

June 1978 – Ernesto Cortissoz International Airport, Barranquilla, Colombia, South America, en route to Miami International Airport, Florida, United States of North America.

My father's sister, Tia Matilda, and her daughter Magdalena had flown from Bogota a couple of days earlier to spend time with us. It was a certainty that our move to the United States was permanent and they wanted to provide support during a difficult time. They waited at the airport for us to board a flight to Miami, Florida. Tia Matilda was a soft-spoken, gentle woman who cared very much for my mother and us. She was a school principal who demonstrated an unbelievable ability to touch the lives of not only her family, but also her students and staff. Tia Matilda humbly exemplified the good nature in humanity. She felt it important we see my father's side of the family in a good light. Her company that day was a testimony of her kindness and love for us. Tia Matilda perked up as she held Mother's hand, "Beatrice, you are a strong person, a strong person! Do not worry, your family in the states will be there to help you." She continued, "I know Octavio is not a bad person. He will come to his senses." Mother gave her a facial expression, a particular look that stated her strong disagreement with what she was hearing. Tia Matilda ignored the look and continued, "I want you to know you are doing the right thing." Mother listened but did not say a word. My parents' relationship had taken a dive and Mother had difficulty dealing with the unpleasant reality of rejection. I still recall explosive fights. Episodes of complete chaos, a few of them rendered Mother emotionally distraught and unable to care for us. It was a volatile situation that brought daily challenges into our home. It was during these very trying times that Tia Matilda had stepped in to fill the void left by my parents' absence. She became a surrogate caretaker to my brother, Gabriel, and me. Although she was patient and loving, she was not able to shelter us entirely from the absolute madness in our home, which had culminated in my parents' separation.

I knew I would miss my loving aunt but could not wait to leave my parents' house of terror. I had suffered from horrific, unceasing nightmares. The nightmare was always the same. Sometimes when I closed my eyes, I can still clearly see the man dressed in a white long robe, like the kind priest wear. Night after night, he would walk in the door of my bedroom and stand near the foot of my bed. I felt his manifestation but was too scared to look at his face. He would always walk a couple of steps toward the window, swiftly move the sheer curtains to the side and look out into the darkness of the night. He would then briefly turn toward me. I felt his look piercing through me, taunting me, his unmistakable presence waking me out of a deep sleep in the middle of the night. I recognized him to be a bad presence, although he claimed to be God. He communicated with me and I would threaten, "Leave my room or I will tell my parents!"

Calmly and with a cynical voice as if to dare me, he would respond, "Go ahead, tell them." I would scream uncontrollably, as loud as I could. My screams were followed by Mother and Father's abrupt run to my room. The light immediately flicked on, Mother would hug me as Father would take me in his arms and carry me to their bedroom.

Sometimes I was taunted while asleep in between my parents and I would see him sitting at the foot of their bed. He knew I could see him and he didn't care. Every night I went to bed in a complete panic because I knew it was a certainty that he would return to grace me with his unpleasant visit.

Mother thought our house was possessed and wanted to call a priest. She never did go to a church. Instead, she visited numerous witchdoctors. A woman who was an expert in white magic told her that Father's lover had placed a curse on us because she wanted to rid us out of Father's life. Mother believed this, and I might have too. The woman was a medium who claimed to work miracles through the power of archangels, who are believed to be warriors against evil. She visited with the purpose of exorcising the malicious spirit that dwelled in our home and bring my nightmares to an end. It did not stop, and now I was relieved Mother had decided to leave the wicked place.

Cousin Magdalena was much older than I. I had spent a significant amount of time in her house and we had become close. I considered her an older sister. She was protective and caring. Magdalena was a university student studying business. She also did volunteer work at Tia Matilda's foundation, a schoolhouse for impoverished children. She had a demanding schedule and very little spare time. She demonstrated that she valued me and loved me when she requested special permission from her university professors to take a few days off and traveled to Barranquilla. She was a compassionate, pretty young lady who knew it was a vulnerable time. She knew her schoolwork would pile up but wanted to spend time with me before our departure.

Cousin Magdalena dressed prim, and kept her mid-length black hair well groomed. Her caramel colored eyes combined beautifully with her olive colored skin and lovely smile. Magdalena was down to earth, and didn't act like the only daughter of wealthy parents. She enjoyed a privileged life but was humble, well-mannered and kind to everyone. I appreciated her presence at the airport as she helped me feel relaxed about the trip. I remember I believed her when she gave me a warm embrace and said "Josefina, do not worry. Everything will be all right." I hoped we would still be able to stay in touch with one another but I knew everything was about to change. She had explained that my parents' troubles had nothing to do with me and I should just be a kid and not pay any mind to adult problems. I understood she was right but I was about to lose my surrogate mother, the woman who had allowed me to be a kid. I felt burdened and responsible for mother and Gabriel. I had no cushion to help me withstand the blow of a parent who seemed frail. I could tell my mother felt insecure and did not know how she would start all over without Father.

I had struggled in school and was performing very poorly. My grades were below average and here I was about to go to a country where the language was foreign to me. I was certain it meant I would fail altogether. There were so many unanswered questions in my head. Would I make friends? Will the kids at my new school think I'm weird? Since I had no recollection of my kindergarten year, I wondered if I could learn English before kids would start to make fun of me. I asked myself, "How do kids dress there? Where would we live?" With so many unanswered questions, I realized my problems were much more than my parents' separation; I was personally afraid.

My parents' fighting had culminated with Mother packing our bags, abandoning all our belongings and booking one-way tickets to Barranquilla. We had left Bogota two weeks earlier because Mother mistakenly thought it would be a wake-up call for Father. She wanted him to follow us to Barranquilla to demonstrate he loved us and wanted us in his life. The plan had not worked. Instead, she realized leaving for good was our only choice. Mother's family had migrated to the United States and now we sought refuge with them.

We walked out the airport's departure lounge onto an outdoor gate. After a few steps on the runway and a moment before climbing the steps to board the airplane, Mother said to us, "Take a deep breath, smell your surroundings. You don't know how long it will be before we return to this country." Seeing the sadness in her face was difficult to bear. She felt defeated, forced out of our home, and it pained her.

The smell of kerosene permeated the warm, humid, tropical air. I felt nauseous and torn. Things had not gone well for us in Colombia, nevertheless, the opportunity of a fresh start allowed a nervous excitement to accompany this gloomy journey.

Mother had become obsessed with my father, Octavio. He had systematically conducted endless disappearing acts, betraying her with countless women. He had finally settled for one lover and was openly living a double life as the head of two families. I never understood why he rejected Mother. She was gorgeous, and was received with admiration wherever we would go. I often heard people compare her physical appearance to that of Sophia Loren. I'd often notice people around us showering her with attention. I heard a man call her "universally beautiful," as he took off his hat and bowed to her. Others, less brave, quietly glanced as she walked by. Mother was tall and thin, but curvy. She had cat-shaped eyes with high cheekbones and a defined jawline. When she smiled, her red, voluminous lips would strikingly reveal her even, white teeth. She was the most beautiful woman in the world. What was most troubling to me was that my stunning mother, who was almost ten years younger than my father, loved him so passionately despite his incorrigible behavior. Father was a thirty-year-old widow whose wife had died of lupus. Mother was a nineteen-year-old who fantasized about love. She immediately took to Father's advances and married him after a short four months of courtship. She wanted to take on the responsibilities of stepmother to his son, but their maternal aunt had made a commitment to Father that she would raise him. He made the decision not to bring him into his new marriage because he believed he had grown accustomed to his aunt's home. He felt the boy had suffered enough loss and did not think it wise to destabilize him. She tried to be the wife she thought Father wanted, but he took no notice of her efforts. He was always busy gallivanting, leaving her lonely and desperate.

The decision to leave Colombia was far from abrupt. Mother fought hard to keep her family together. The straw that broke the camel's back was when Mother was diagnosed with ovarian cancer. It had been caught during the earliest stage 1 Phase, affecting one ovary. Fortunately, her doctor was able to stop the disease's progression before it could spread by surgically removing the ovary, along with the damaged cells. A dose of radiation therapy was given to her to help prevent a recurrence. I did not understand much but was told she had been successfully put in remission.

As Mother lay in a hospital bed, my father traveled throughout Europe with his lover. Air France and British Airways had built twenty Concorde turbojet airliners and he was one of the first thousand privileged passengers to travel in one of the Concorde's commercial flights. For his accomplishment, he purchased a commemorative gold medallion. As if the universe revolved around him, he bragged about the gold medallion he had obtained from Air France, "This commemorates the first thousand passengers to experience the Concorde's service flights. It is an engineering marvel..." I was too young to understand this made him a complete jackass. For mother, this would be the final, indisputable indication that it was time to leave.

Her illness had put her in a depressed state. She had experienced multiple meltdowns while trying to keep her marriage together. She had clearly been defeated, and reuniting with her family in the United States was the only option we had at that point.

I was looking forward to better times. I prayed all the misery was behind us. I understood staying in Colombia would be the death of my mother, but still I could not help the nostalgic feeling that crept in as I followed Mother's instructions and breathed deep while I prayed it wouldn't be so long before we returned. Insecure and scared, I looked back, hoping to take the last glimpse of cousin Magdalena. I scanned the area by the gate but there was no sign of her. Disappointed, I put a foot forward, walking into the jumbo jet, Boeing 747.

We were assigned the middle, which held four seats per row. Mother chose to sit next to the gentleman on the end and allowed Gabriel and I to sit next to one another. I couldn't see out the window so I decided to play "Name That Tune" with Gabriel until the flight took off. It was a smooth flight. The man sitting next to Mother did not quiet for a single moment. She was polite, but obviously disinterested. Upon landing in Miami, Florida, he confessed he was not a good traveler, and talking was a way of distracting his fears. Mother assured him it was no inconvenience. He shared that he was vacationing so she wished him a good stay and signaled Gabriel and I to move out into the aisle so we could disembark.

Customs, Miami International Airport

"Kids, stay close to me. Let him go over to the other line," said Mother. "Him" was the stranger who had spent the last two and a half hours sitting next to Mother. He was the same chatterbox that did not allow anyone to get any rest during the flight. In the airplane she did not have a choice but to engage in conversation but at customs she drew the line. She did not like his nervous energy. She

16

was cautious and did not trust any stranger flying out of Colombia, and certainly did not trust any affiliation with a stranger flying out of Colombia and arriving at the United States customs. Mother stated things had changed as if she needed to give Gabriel and me an excuse to stay away from the stranger. She said, "A few years ago your grandmother, Mami Abuela, traveled here with a parrot in hand and quesito Colombiano, arequipe, bocadillos, and no one cared. Now, if you bring extra luggage, they keep you in customs for hours.

After her command, we obediently stepped away from the stranger. As if fearing getting lost in the immigration department, we glued ourselves next to Mother. To an eight-year-old girl, the customs officers looked stern and intimidating. I felt my mother's uneasiness. He looked at her passport and read her name out loud, Beatrice Lopez; she nodded, indicating yes. He asked if we were transporting any goods or monies in excess of ten thousand dollars that needed to be declared. Mother responded with a firm no. Her seriousness gave me the impression that these were dangerous times for Colombians traveling to the States. Our baggage was thoroughly checked and our passports were stamped. "Welcome back to the United States," said the customs agent.

Mother replied in her broken English, "Thank you, sir," and under her breath in Spanish, "Un lugar que nunca debimos haber dejado."

Our arrival at the Miami Airport was circumstantial. We walked slowly past the well-lit, duty-free shop. I noticed the beautifully displayed merchandise. There were elegant dresses, some jewelry, and trays of make-up, not far from the numerous liquor bottles. The smell of perfumes was subtle and inviting. It already felt like a new place. The airport in Barranquilla was small and did not have such fancy stores. We continued to walk over to another terminal where we would board a connecting flight to our final destination, New York City, New York.

Shortly after arriving at the terminal we boarded the plane. It was a fairly quick and uneventful flight. I sat in my assigned

seat, fastened my seatbelt, and barely had a chance to play with my tray-table before I fell fast asleep.

CHAPTER 2

New York City

A little over two and a half hours later I woke up as the plane landed at John F. Kennedy International Airport in Jamaica, Queens, New York. We disembarked and slowly walked toward the gate. I was still half asleep when I suddenly noticed very enthusiastic people waving at us by the security area. Mother smiled and said, "There they are." It took me a moment before I realized it was my grandmother, Mami Abuela, my aunt, Tia Maria, and my uncle, Tio Cesar, who waved cheerful at us by arrivals. As we passed security, they ran toward us, arms wide open. It was nice to get so many enthusiastic hugs and kisses. It felt as if I was meeting everyone for the first time. We had spent a long year and a half in Colombia and during that time I had lost the image of our family in New York.

Mami Abuela had a full head of white hair. She had given birth to nine children and experienced the misfortune of eleven miscarriages. Apparently, the woman never experienced a period in her adult life. She claimed the god of fertility blessed her with many pregnancies after merely smelling my grandfather, Papi Abuelo's, underwear. She proudly stated, "Papi Abuelo has never seen me naked! He once made an attempt while I was showering but it was in vain and he learned never to try it again." Everyone found this absurd claim comical while I really believed the god of fertility had not just blessed her but had transformed her into a human incubator.

It was said that Tio David, the youngest of mother's siblings, was born weighing sixteen pounds. He was a celebrated anomaly among the doctors and nurses at the hospital the day of his birth. Jokes were made about how Tio David entered school shortly after Mami Abuela and he were discharged from the maternity ward. It was unusual, even for women in her era, to be so fertile but Mami Abuela was far from a common woman – she was a matriarch.

Although she spoke of the god of fertility, she was a devout Catholic. That day at the airport she wore a green dress, a demonstration of faith to Saint Jude in gratitude for answering her prayer for our safe return to America. She was always praying for something or mourning over someone's death. She was a seamstress who made her own dresses. Her wardrobe consisted mainly of multiple black and green outfits. Mami Abuela had a soft spot for the indigent, lonely souls with no families. She cried at the sight of injustice and was always first to protect those in need. Mami Abuela was a true underdog superhero. If a person in the vicinity died with no one to mourn for him or her, Mami Abuela voluntarily paid homage. She attended strangers' funerals like it was her job because she felt every human, no matter rich or poor, young or old, good or bad, deserved to go on to eternal life with dignity. Her daughters would jokingly say she was a sort of unpaid crier for hire at local funeral homes. She did not care. She was thankful for all her blessings and the good fortune of having nine healthy children and twenty-four amazing grandchildren. It was her small way to give back. Mami Abuela wore green dresses to publicly demonstrate her reverence and gratitude for Saint Jude's miraculous work. That day at the airport she hugged me tight. I bumped against her big, round belly and I remember innocently asking her if she was expecting a baby. She thought it was a hilarious question and pretended to scold me, "Don't be imprudent, you curious little girl, caramba!" while laughing loudly.

Tia Maria, one of mother's younger sisters, gave me a warm snuggle, and it felt inexplicably pleasant, as if we had never been apart. She looked at me and said, "Oh my, same sassy Josefina! Love you so much." I was almost six years old when I last saw her and couldn't clearly remember her, but I immediately connected to this obviously sweet lady. She stood a little over five feet tall and was on the thin side. Her tan complexion was flawless and she did not need to wear much make-up. She had put on just the right amount of mascara, which accentuated her pretty brown eyes. She laughed with a wide-open mouth that let out a musical sound contagious to anyone who would hear her, and eye-catching because of her perfectly white teeth. Her husband, Tio Cesar, had shoulder length hair with soft curls, a handsome Argentinian man who loved the Beatles. He wore a button-down shirt and fitted pants. His accent was different than ours. He spoke a European Spanish, which sounded like the Castilian of northern and central Spain. He flaunted a sophisticated confidence and noticeably stylish demeanor. His elegance was hard to ignore, similar to that of a movie star. Tio Cesar and Tia Maria were young and made an attractive couple.

We walked toward baggage claim. I was now fully awake and thrilled to see a family I couldn't fully recognize but felt completely comfortable with. The enormous airport's baggage claim area was an exciting place for a kid. There were so many people walking around and there were signs written in English everywhere. Ecstatically, I skipped my way around. I had arrived at a truly new and bigger world. I felt a boost of energy after the melancholic departure from the small airport in Barranquilla. We gathered our luggage and walked outside. I was looking forward to buying an American Milky Way chocolate bar at a local store rather than waiting for someone to gift it when visiting Colombia from the States.

Tio Cesar drove a Fiat but had borrowed an Oldsmobile to make sure he could fit our luggage and all of us in "the big car." Driving off the airport curb in the darkness of the night, four of us squeezing in the back seat, that night felt... adventurous!

As I gazed out the back window of the borrowed Oldsmobile, I felt rapt by the concentration of well-lit skyscrapers, visible across the impressive Whitestone Bridge. The clear night sky displayed an intimidating and enchanting view of New York City that evening. Tio Cesar drove into northern Manhattan and dropped us off in front of a five story high tenement. It had distinctive ornamentation on the roof, enhancing the stone structure in Washington Heights. We walked up the cement steps and in through double glass black metal frame doors. We entered the building. Everyone, still excited about the reunion, waited for the elevator. "Oh gross! That is the biggest roach I've ever seen!" I screamed. My mother scolded me and I felt a bit pretentious. Everyone quieted and looked at me. Tia Maria held a half smile on her face. I couldn't understand how such a filthy thing could be ignored but I was about to find out.

Walking into Mami Abuela's apartment shook all the delight out of the reunion. The lengthy, dim hallway obviously did not get the benefit of any ventilation. The smell of cigarettes accompanied by the foggy-like air from the heavy cigarette smoke and dingy walls made for a depressing first impression. After the awkwardness in the elevator, I thought it best to stay quiet. The hallway connected to several rooms.

At the end there was an opening to the left leading to the entrance of the ill-decorated living room. The left wall by the entrance had dark brown, wooden panels. I was certain the panels served to house the giant roaches that dwelled in this building. Evidently there had been an attempt to decorate the wall on the right. A series of circular designs made of stucco had been plastered on the wall. Each circle had a jutting, sharp, pointy, weapon-like end that demanded caution. This strange quasi three-dimensional image was an unattractive contributor to the impression of chaos and disarray that sent a chill down my neck.

The five-bedroom apartment was one of a kind in so far as its size. It was one of the few big apartments left in New York City. Sadly, the fact that four families lived there stole its charm. I knew it had only been a year and a half but this all seemed new to me. Perhaps having experienced a wealthy lifestyle in Colombia made me see everything differently. I was a bit older and felt an immense disappointment as my fantasies about life in America were shattered.

Overwhelmed, I glanced at Mother who did not acknowledge my disappointment. She struggled to keep herself from any discouraging feelings and demonstrated gratitude to be among her loving family. She smiled and hugged everyone in the apartment. Everyone spoke over each other's voices and laughed loudly. There was a sense of disorganization that no one but me seemed to notice.

Mother's indifference gave me the impression that she had grown up in this chaos and its familiarity kept her from any disheartened emotions. Mother would later share with me that she found strength in the knowledge that it was a temporary transition that would ultimately lead to her liberation from our troubled life in Colombia. Later that night Mami Abuela began her nightly routine; a rosary prayer, accompanied by ten Hail Marys and Our Fathers, followed by the lighting of a white candle for all the saints, a red one for the Sacred Heart of Jesus, and a green one for Saint Jude. She taught me that as a symbol of humility before God's mercy and reverence, I should kneel down near her bed, fold my hands in a position for prayer, look at the images of the crucifix and the saints in her alter, and profess my faith.

After the final prayer, we were accommodated as best as was possible. Two mattresses were laid on the living room floor. The arrangement was uncomfortable. Looking around the disorganized, gloomy apartment I wondered if this might be worse than Colombia's misery. I remembered our beautifully landscaped lawn and house, our nice cars, my nanny, and the ladies that kept our home clean. I remembered the forest behind our home where we played hide and seek with our neighborhood friends. I thought of the fireplace that decorated one of the three living rooms in our house and wished I were not laying on this cold living room floor, surrounded by people I didn't remember. I stopped feeling sorry for myself when I remembered that my mother's sanity and our safety were at stake. I reminded myself of my parents' violent arguments, the terrorizing sleepless nights, the sadness in my mother's eyes, her absence in our lives, the disease that could have caused her death... and just like that, in an instant, this new world became bearable. I let a quiet tear run down my face, said my prayers, and kissed my mom goodnight.

CHAPTER 3

A few days later, Mother got a job at the shawl factory where my aunts worked. She was earning five cents for every shawl she attached to a wooden ring. My mother was glad to be able to start working immediately. She wanted to be a strong woman, to prove that she was up for the challenge of starting a new life.

Motivated by the thought of moving out of Mami Abuela's house, she worked long hours. She put wooden rings on shawls faster than anyone had ever seen at that factory. Her first paycheck was $240.00. It didn't seem like enough to her so she worked harder. Soon, she was consistently earning $300.00 weekly. The best part of her new job was that she brought the shawls that didn't make the cut home for me to wear. The shawls were not perfect but they were colorful, sparkling, some fringed, and some were crocheted. There was an array of beautiful, voguish shawls, including some cape-style solid colored ones. I especially loved the long black shawls made out of silk. I pretended they were wigs and wore them on my head all day long. I also rolled up socks in the shape of balls then stuff them in my t-shirt by my chest area. I pretended to be a sophisticated New Yorker, with long, silky smooth black hair and big breasts. I didn't own a bra and had never worn one, so it was difficult to keep the socks in place. Half the time I would run around, chasing after Gabriel with a single big breast and half a flat chest. My cousins mocked me but I didn't care. At the time, owning a shawl was an extravagant fashion statement, and I owned several shawls so this made me a stylish, worldly girl no matter what they said. I claimed to be a real Disco queen while running and fighting over toys. My cousins called me the tomboy with a wig. I poked fun back and everyone laughed together. We called it "snap wars". In the end, we all made the best of having to share a small space in a "big" apartment. The cousins, Gabriel and I understood the dangers of growing up in a big city and, although we argued against one another, outside the apartment we understood the importance of sticking together and protecting one another in this place we called home.

Playing childhood fantasies with Gabriel and my cousins diverted my attention away from the adult troubles in Colombia and toward the business of being a real kid. Mami Abuela's house was not such a bad place after all. It was overcrowded with people who were unconcerned with riches. Happiness came from enjoying life as it was, slowly diminishing the worries of Mother's pains and building a new trouble-free life.

Everyone looked forward to the traditional weekend family parties. Celebrating and forgetting about the week's hard work had become routine, which always involved music and dancing. I loved listening to traditional Colombian songs; it reminded me of our home in Bogota. I had many favorite musicians, like Nelson Enrique, Palito Ortega, Joe Arroyo, Diomedes Diaz, Rafael Escalona, Fonseca, Pacho Galan, Billos's Caracas Boys, along with some others. We played the same records over and over. Everyone knew the lyrics, and we sang loudly and danced together. The neighborhood was made up of primarily Spanish families, so no one really complained about the noise since everyone seemed to enjoy the same mindset. To be part of a close community of people with similar interest was so much fun.

Within a short amount of time I had settled into my grandparents' house. To my delight, the frequent nightmares I experienced in Colombia had miraculously stopped and I felt love and appreciation for everyone, especially Tia Maria. She took care of all the kids while all the other sisters worked at the factory. My grandfather, Papi

Abuelo, was playful and tolerant to the many grandchildren that ran around the apartment. We were a total of ten cousins playing in the apartment as if it was a park, all fighting over everything, including the right to choose which programing to watch on the one small television. There was a choice of about five channels. Although we all wanted to watch the same Tom and Jerry cartoons, we were kids who simply enjoyed arguing. We had brawls over gaining control of the TV, which became one the most amusing games for us kids and one of the most irritating things for Tia Maria.

Papi Abuelo followed a very specific daily routine. He worked the afternoon shift at the American Book Company and took advantage of the morning hours to get ready for work. Every morning he would cook red Goya beans and pack the red bean soup for lunch. He habitually ironed a white button shirt and gray slacks. His clothes always looked impeccable. After ironing, he would proceed to boil water in a pot for shaving purposes. He would use the same tin cup and fill it with the boiling water from the stove. I can still see him walk toward the bathroom while calling out loudly, "Coming through, the water is hot, hot, hot, hot, hot! Watch out! Coming through!" and every day, systematically, we'd hear him say, "Darn it! These kids are always in the way! Maria, you better talk to their mothers about an alternative day care, I'm tired of getting burned every day!" We suspected he didn't mean it because a long loutish fart almost always followed his statements. We took no offense. We thought it was very amusing. He would always crack a smile, holding back the laughter as he commonly said, "What is all the raucous over? It's just a little gas."

Tia Maria would grow so desperate that she'd try to punish us by ordering us to kneel down facing the long hallway walls. We thought her tactics were entertaining. We knew she did not have a single mean bone in her. She would catch us being rambunctious and would go to consequence number two, demand we kneel while keeping our hands raised and arms up in the air, so to make sure we weren't touching one another. Ten out of ten times we continued to carry on. She would always go forward with her final consequence, a very alarmed walk through the hallway, a frying pan in hand, fearlessly used to give each one of us a swift knock on the head. An intense ringing in our brains, without fail, prompted the nonsense to a halt. Her disciplinary ways were somewhat painful, but mostly comical. For the most part, the sight of the frying pan was enough of a deterrent. A few times she used it with little to no force. Tia Maria was outnumbered by a bunch of tumultuous kids who took advantage of every opportunity to drive her near insanity. She was a sweet, loving momma bear who would never do anything to hurt us.

It was still summer and in New York City this meant the ice-cream truck frequently rolled around the neighborhood, playing a familiar jingle, enticing the neighborhood kids to chase after it. The moment we heard the familiar song, my cousins, Gabriel, and I ran out of the apartment. We'd jump as quickly as possible down several steps at a time to reach the first floor. Whoever got to the ice cream truck first was in charge of holding it up for the rest to get there. The ice cream truck runs created one of my fondest memories of Papi Abuelo. I could still see him gesturing to get my attention. In a silent effort to sneak me away from the other grandchildren, he waved his arms, pointing in the direction of the front door. He wanted to buy ice cream just for me. That afternoon, Papi Abuelo confirmed what I had always suspected, that he secretly favored me. As the ice cream truck systematic rolled around the block doing marathon runs, Papi Abuelo kept buying. He bought me a record-breaking four chocolate and vanilla swirls with chocolate sprinkles. It was crazy. I guess he wanted to do something special for me. Surprisingly, I refused the fifth cone, which might have been what saved me from a visit to the emergency room.

That evening as I complained of terrible stomach pains, Mother said to me, "Your grandpa has always had a weak spot for you. I will have to speak to him about not spoiling you this way." Relieved that Mother seemed amused by my grandfather's silly attempt to show favoritism and forgetting I was feeling sick, I noticed she had a smile on her face and had lost some of the sadness in her eyes. I did not ask her why she seemed happy. I was afraid to ruin her good mood, so I kept it to myself.

We lay on our mattress later that night. Mother enthusiastically told me she had found a new home for us. "Josefina, tomorrow we'll go see an apartment that is up for rent."

"Really? I'm so happy. Did you see it?"

"No! Not yet. I wanted to see it with you and Gabriel," she said. I was so proud of Mother. She was a superhero in my eyes. In a few months' time she was able to execute her plan of relocating us to a new home in the United States. She put her earnings, along with the one thousand dollars in savings she brought from Colombia, and had managed to come up with enough money to move us out of Mami Abuela's congested apartment.

I was glad to leave, but only because of one of my aunts. Tia Ana lived in one of the rooms at the apartment. She was a bitter woman, mother of my cousins Lucy and James, who lost her husband to a fatal heart attack during her eighth month of pregnancy with Lucy. Her resentfulness about the cards life had dealt her turned her into a rancorous person who adopted the attitude that the world was against her. She was mean and ill spirited toward me. Tia Ana felt sorry for herself and her children, and embodied the "poor me" belief, and had put up a wall against the world. The mindset that everyone was against her and her orphan children blinded her. She carried on her pity party for so long, and she misconstrued all the circumstances around her. She could not understand that my cousins and I clowned around and sometimes we playfully argued. It didn't mean we hated one another. She often spanked me and accused me of hurting her children who were slightly younger than I was. I really did not like her but I tried to respect her. I can still remember the time when Lucy and I were playing tug of war with a towel. She walked into the room and violently slapped a tooth out of my mouth. Gabriel cried while I bled profusely.

Tia Maria was protective of Gabriel and I. Alarmed by the blood on my clothes, she held me as she questioned Tia Ana's unacceptable attack. They engaged in a screaming match and, as luck would have it, Mother arrived from work in the midst of the disturbing episode. A terrible confrontation between mother and Tia Ana erupted. Tia Ana picked up sharp scissors lying next to Mami Abuela's SINGER and attempted to stab Mother. Horrified, I watched Mami Abuela get in the way of her viciousness, thankfully halting a possible tragedy. Afterward, Mother took Gabriel and me for a long walk. She was visibly upset and frustrated. I felt responsible and promised myself I would stay far away from Tia Ana.

Mami Abuela's house was everyone's house and we didn't have any special rights or privileges. Mother and Tia Ana's animosity toward one another had been brewing. Mother was aware of Tia Ana's abusive behavior toward me. Since we arrived from Colombia she had ignored several incidents but could not contain herself any longer. Now the line had been crossed and she was afraid the hostilities were too high to continue living together. To avoid additional conflicts, Mother opted to accelerate our move out.

CHAPTER 4

The next day after work Mother took my brother and me to an apartment building about ten blocks away from Mami Abuela's place in Washington Heights. In July, New York sits on the surface of the sun; walking in the unbearable heat made me feel lethargic and sweaty. It was a disappointment to walk in a building and realize there was no elevator. Just as I was about to protest, I remembered I didn't want to be near Tia Ana any longer. She had made an otherwise fine experience very unpleasant. I thought, "Oh no! I'm melting!" and quietly proceeded with the laborious climb up five levels.

I was dripping with sweat when we entered the three-bedroom one-bathroom apartment on the fifth floor. We walked into a hallway with a bedroom on the left near the front door, followed by a bathroom and the kitchen, which were all on the left side as well. The kitchen had the most uninviting light yellow colored wallpaper. Nonetheless, it certainly beat the stucco walls at Mami Abuela's house. It had a small window with a view of a courtyard, a stove, double ceramic sinks, two cupboards and a refrigerator. Our own refrigerator! I took a peek out the window and walked out into the hallway. The living room was at the end of the hallway and it opened to two additional bedrooms. The main bedroom had very appealing grand windows that faced an avenue bustling with the energy of a crowded city. We could see all the way across the road to the heavy activity of people and car traffic weaving at intersections. The third bedroom was ordinary except for the window that opened to what would become my favorite place, the fire escape. The walls throughout most of the apartment were painted white and there was enough closet space for our few belongings. I thought climbing the steps was a small price to pay for this perfect place, and everyone agreed.

Mother had started a new democratic system in which we were allowed to vote on any and all significant decisions necessary in our lives. A majority vote ruled and we would proceed accordingly. As I matured I came to understand this was Mother's way of disguising her inability to make decisions or accept responsibility for the outcome of her choices. The solution to her shortcomings was to instill a system that would divide the liability equally among Gabriel, she, and me. Maybe she thought if we all assumed the load, then we could divide the consequences equally and the outcome wouldn't be so insufferable. That day Gabriel, mother and me unanimously voted yes on taking that apartment. To this day I love that place!

A week later we spent our first and most memorable night in our new place. The inauguration came accompanied by the unforgettable experience of a gang shooting. Gabriel and I saw the action from the start.

Earlier that evening we were taking a work break from the tiresome move. Still feeling mesmerized by the grand window, we sat and watched the people and the traffic on the busy street. Captivated by the sound of the beeping horns, the neighborhood kids playing outside, the lit up storefront signs, we lost track of time. We suddenly noticed a male figure running in the dark, heading west toward our building. Mid-block he desperately sought shelter down steps that led to a basement. No one would ever see that man run again. Later, chalk outlined a body that laid lifeless, posing for a forensic photographer. He was probably a small-time thug who did not merit a mention on the news or a few lines in the local paper.

By the next morning, the chalk figure, like the victim, was invisible, erased. Yet, for that night, he was the protagonist of the homicide investigation, visible through our very own movie theater screen/bedroom window. We witnessed the NYPD in action; similar to a great Kojak episode, several police units illuminated the streets with blue and red piercing lights. Numerous uniformed officers and officials in suits paced the scene of the crime and captivated the local residents. The curiosity Gabriel and I felt was thrilling. I loved Kojak so the events were entertaining and not at all scary. Our arrival into what would become the place that holds my dearest lifetime memories had indeed the magic only a child could appreciate. Despite the homicide, I felt happy. Happy my mother looked happy. Happy we didn't have to share one bathroom with four other families. Happy my dad was not making my mom cry, or my mom wasn't fighting with my dad, or my mom was not depressed. I was happy to have our own home, our own refrigerator. Just happy.

Summer was over. Gabriel and I started at the local public school. Mrs. Smith, my teacher, was wonderful but that year was difficult for me. Although my parents had lived in New York before our move to Colombia, it had severely interfered with my English language proficiency. Spanish is my mother tongue and I was only at the end of my Kindergarten year when we returned to Colombia. Sadly, I had forgotten all I had learned and now I did not understand a single word in the English language. The teacher pointed at a picture of a spoon and called out my name so I could name the object and spell the word "spoon". I was unable to say a word. It prompted the class bully to pick on me day after day. As time passed, he expanded his abusive repertoire. He thought my clothes did not meet the standard either. Mother was so busy working that she did not realize our clothes were too small and that Gabriel and I wore clothes that we had outgrown. Our tight high-water pants and our sneakers were from a bargain store. Most of my new friends did not notice, but this one kid in particular made it his job to poke fun at me. This unpleasant experience was a direct consequence of my innate inability to mind my own business. Sticking up for another student against a bully had a price. The bully simply transferred his persecution onto me and I had allowed this to go on for many months.

One morning I asked Mrs. Smith for permission to use the restroom. She said no, and sent me back to my seat. I really needed to go so I reluctantly walked back to my seat. Without noticing, as I was about to sit, the bully pulled my seat out from under me. I fell flat on my behind and to my complete humiliation, I peed myself. I was devastated! All the students in the class noticed the puddle of pee on the floor. They chuckled and stared at me with complete disbelief as I cried inconsolably. I could barely get myself to look up at the rest of the class. Mrs. Smith sent me to the nurse's office with a note. The nurse called Mami Abuela's house and Tia Maria rushed to the school with a change of clothes. I couldn't get myself to walk back in the classroom that day. The teacher spoke to Tia Maria and they decided it would be best for me to go home.

My teacher had finally noticed the bully's behavior and made every effort to protect me. That evening Mrs. Smith phoned Mother and a meeting was set up for the next day. The following morning before class began, Mother attended the meeting. I felt comfortable enough to confess to being the victim of a bully. I had stayed quiet to spare Mother the grief but I had routinely dealt with being pushed and pulled by this boy and could no longer bear to keep quiet. He used lies to convince his mother that I was bullying him. The mother never arranged to meet with Mrs. Smith's regarding the matter. Instead, she confronted me outside the school building several times with harsh words.

That morning during the parent-teacher school meeting. I cried loudly, "That boy is mean and ignorant. His mother treated me harshly several times in the front of the school building." Accusing the boy was the smartest thing I ever did. Mother knew I was telling the truth. She worked long hours and knew she could not protect me because she was unable to pick Gabriel and me up after school. She sensed my desperation and immediately withdrew my brother and me from the public school. Mother spoke to me about my outgoing personality, "Josefina, just tame yourself, fly under the radar so you don't attract so much negative attention. You have a beautiful personality but people sometimes misunderstand others. Just going forward, try to avoid trouble whenever possible." Mother believed I was too outspoken and that people perceived me to be a menace. I wanted to be socially disciplined but I was spiritually free and could not change my nature. Mother often stated I was like the cartoon character, Underdog, defender of the weak, ready to go to the rescue.

After mother's meeting with Mrs. Smith, we headed straight to the registration office at a nearby Catholic school. Fortunately, they agreed to accept new registrations although we were halfway through the academic year. Mother negotiated a tuition break with the nuns that administrated the parochial school. She registered Gabriel and me immediately, and the next day we were both at the school for attendance. It was Mother's kindest act toward me. I could once again feel safe at school, and I no longer had to watch my back in the cafeteria or deal with the fear of harassing words from a bully and his mother. School became the one place where I could finally just be a kid.

Mami Abuela was an amazing seamstress but I was glad that her homemade clothes would no longer be a source of ammunition for the kids in school to use against me. I wanted to tell Mother that even if I would have been a reserved girl, my outfits made it near impossible for me not to attract anyone's negative attention. I, of course, kept it quiet because I knew mother was working hard and I did not want to add any pressure.

At the parochial school, I felt proud to wear the white school blouse with the green bow tie. It went really well with the knife pleated school skirt or the plaid jumper which showed off a stitched-on school emblem.

As part of the curriculum, students attended mass every Friday. I struggled as an English learner but I was an enthusiastic student who did not mind being called "teacher's pet". My favorite subjects were social studies and religion. My grades improved as I naturally and almost effortlessly acquired English language proficiency. I was a popular student, proud of my love affair with history and God. To this day I remain eternally grateful for the parochial school's protection. It not only provided a safe haven for my brother and me, but it also allowed me to experience religion in a very personal way.

Teachers knew most of the kids at the school were disadvantaged and treated their students as if they were their own children. This was proven through the numerous acts of kindness toward the student body. I experienced my teacher's generosity on a first hand basis when Gabriel stole a Blow Pop lollipop from the display counter at the corner store and walked out without paying. The grocery store owner held my brother back and demanded our phone number so he could call our mother. I ran back to my classroom and told my homeroom teacher, Mrs. Murphy, what had happened. Without hesitation, she grabbed her coat and followed me to the grocery store. She was a caring woman who truly wanted all her students to succeed. She walked down a couple of steps and went into the small grocery store. Acting more like a mother than my teacher, she held Gabriel's hand instead of scolding him, paid the grocery man ten cents, and walked out. She took him back to the classroom where she asked if we were hungry. Gabriel was embarrassed so he responded with a quiet "No." She was not judgmental when she gently reminded him that doing the right thing was an important part of being a good man and that taking something without paying for it was considered stealing, although she knew he had done it innocently. She proceeded to hug him and sent us home. I was fortunate to have a kind-hearted teacher whom I could trust.

Mrs. Murphy easily could have handled my brother differently that day. I will never forget her infinite compassion, and will always keep her in my heart. I truly believe she significantly contributed to Gabriel's positive view of the world.

Across the street from our school was a beautiful church. It became one of my most beloved places where I always felt a spiritual strength. I thought of Mother every time I looked at the statue of Mary near the altar. The image was comforting, especially when I found myself missing Mother. She was absent, working long hours, but somehow in that church I felt her protection. I enjoyed every moment I was in the sand-colored walls of the enormous building. The stained glass windows adorned and provided light for the numerous sculptures of various Catholic saints. The smell of incense and the peaceful silence provided a second home for me. I became the first alter girl for our church and ended up serving a total of four years; the last two as head alter server. I enjoyed wearing the alb and performing all my duties. I felt honored to present the cruets of water and wine for the priest to pour into the chalice, to ring the altar bell, and be part of the ceremony. At one point I even dreamed of becoming a nun.

The entrance procession gave me an inexplicable sense of belonging. The recessional was a celebration for me, and approaching the altar while the schoolteachers and students were present was never wearisome. I felt flattered to serve mass for my peers. I was diligent in fulfilling every duty from the start through the ending procession.

I undoubtedly believed with all my heart the teachings of the Bible as interpreted by the Catholic church. School and church were wonderful places, my home away from home.

.

CHAPTER 5

Routine had fallen into place and Mother became obsessed with improving herself. She announced she had registered at a university in the Bronx. She explained to Gabriel and me that a college degree would guarantee a better paying job. She conducted one of her classic weekly meetings where she explained her plan and assured us that all our sacrifices would pay off. We were a team living in a democracy. Once again, we voted to support her efforts for the betterment of all of us. Gabriel and I were assigned chores, and together we worked at keeping our home in order while mother spent all her time either at work or in school. Desperately wanting to provide for us, she was out of the house over twelve hours a day, Monday through Friday. The up side of the situation was that Mother's busy schedule allowed Gabriel and I to use our apartment as if it was a park.

Mother's brothers, Tio Andres and Tio David, came over to the house to help us pick up a brown plaid cloth couch Mother had seen next to the outside dumpster. I was looking out the window and could see them walking toward my building. They each had a six-pack of beer in one hand and in the other, Tio Andres had a hose and Tio David had a small cooler. I buzzed them in the building and could hear them yapping and laughing all the way from the first floor. I opened the front door and waited for them to get to the fifth floor. "Hi Tio Andres, hi Tio David."

Tio David responded, "Hey sobrina, what's going on?"

Tio Andres barked an order at me, "Josefina, put the beer in the fridge and get Gabriel so he can hold the building's front door for us."

"Ok, Gabriel! Tio Andres and Tio David need your help."

Tio Andres continued, "Tell Gabriel to get his butt downstairs fast. We'll be right back. Your mother wants us to bring a couch upstairs."

"Ok, Gabriel – now!" Gabriel always seemed ready for anything and before I could finish calling out for him, he ran past me and out the door. Five minutes later I could hear them talking and laughing loudly as they banged the couch against every corner of the staircase. Gabriel kept asking, "You guys want me to help carry it?"

I heard Tio David respond, "Gabriel you go ahead of us, I need you to hold the door of the apartment."

In a loud voice I called out, "Don't worry! I have the door." I could see them struggling to get the couch turned sideways and around the corner of the last flight of stairs.

My uncles were a blast! They made jokes and laughed all the way up the five flights. I finally got to look at the couch. I must admit, it was hard on the eyes but Mother figured it filled the empty living room space, and that was good enough for all of us. After they placed the couch in the living room they went into the kitchen. Dripping sweat, they each grabbed a beer out of the refrigerator. Tio Andres said, "Gabriel, we are taking the hose up to Tar Beach. Go to my house and get the beach chairs that are right in front of the door."

Gabriel was very excited. Tar Beach was a forbidden placed located on the rooftop of our building. Gabriel smiled and asked, "Where are your house keys?"

Before he could finish asking the question, Tio Andres threw the keys at him. "Hurry up! I'm hot."

"Ok! I'll be right back."

I looked at the old couch in the living room. At first I thought it was ugly but it actually decorated the room nicely. I now thought it didn't look so bad. It was in decent shape and, more importantly, it was light and easily moved so it would not be in the way of our playing space in the living room. I went on to my bedroom window because I wanted to check up on Gabriel. I could see him running back from Tio Andres's apartment building. There were no cars coming but I noticed he crossed the street without looking. I opened the window and screamed, "Hey Gabriel! You should look out for cars before you cross the street!" He heard me loud and clear and I know this because he looked up and gave me the finger. I couldn't believe it! I was trying to be a good sister and he was so nasty in return. "I'm telling Mom when she gets home!" He laughed as if he did not care. That made me really mad so I went to the front door and waited for him to come up. As soon as he got near me, I pushed him. "You are so stupid! Don't you ever give me the finger again! You understand?"

"Hey! You're not my mother, leave me alone."

Tio David said, "You two better stop! Gabriel, I'm throwing the hose down from the roof. I need you to grab it and attach it to the tap in the kitchen."

"What are you guys doing? He's too skinny to dangle out the window."

41

"He's gotta learn to be a man. We need water to cool down the tar on the roof. It's sizzling up there!"

Gabriel didn't care why he wanted him to do it so he immediately agreed, "Ok! I got it!" Tio David put six beers in the small cooler and covered it with the little bit of ice from two ice cube trays we had in the freezer. They headed up to the roof. I held on to Gabriel's t-shirt as he stuck his body halfway out the kitchen window in an effort to look up for the hose. He turned and looked at me, "Let go of my shirt!"

"No way!" I remember looking at his little body and said, "You're too skinny! The only big thing you have is your empty head! The wind can knock you out the window and down five flights! Is that what you want?"

He turned and looked at me, "Stop it! You're so weird!" I didn't care or listen to his disapproval; I was his big sister and I knew better. Suddenly, I saw the hose dangle in front of us. Gabriel got so happy, "I got it! I see it!" He was so thrilled you'd think he just won the lottery or something.

"Be careful! Let it come closer before you go to grab the hose."

Tio Andres said, "Hold on! I'll get it close to the building wall."

It swung in front of us a few times before Gabriel gripped it and confirmed, "Got it!"

"Ok, attach it to the faucet and run the cold water." Gabriel obediently did it. I could hear the water run through the nozzle and up to the hose. "Wow! Good job Gabriel!"

"This is probably the stupidest thing ever! If you're going up to the roof you better be careful!" Gabriel ignored me so I asked him, "Why do you need the hose?"

Gabriel was annoyed by my over protection but still answered, "I think they're going to hose down the roof because the tar gets really hot. I'm grabbing a towel and going up with them."

"OK, I'll be up in a bit too." I didn't want to be up on the roof but I felt I had to protect Gabriel. I remember looking at Gabriel's little legs in his corduroy shorts, and his skinny arms in an old white t-shirt.

I felt like his mother, and thought my uncles were too immature to watch if it was too windy for Gabriel to be up on the roof. He went one flight up to the roof and I could hear Tio David say, "Gabriel, leave the cooler there! We're using it as a door stop."

Gabriel noticed the boom box and responded, "Cool! You have music." He laid his towel on the wet tar and sat on it next to Tio David. He couldn't wait to hear all their nasty stories about women. Kool & the Gang's song, "Celebration," was playing on the radio.

Gabriel was about to sit when Tio Andres threw the bottle opener, "Hey kid, get me a beer out of the cooler." Gabriel got up obediently and walked over to the cooler, pulled out the ice-cold beer as he felt refreshed by the dripping cool water drops on his hands as he grabbed the wet bottle. He placed the bottle between his knees, held onto the top with his right hand, and with his left he popped the top off the bottle. He barely held onto the bottle as he heard the bubbly effervescent sound explosion. A rich malty aroma fizzed out of the top, making it too enticing for Gabriel to resist. He made sure the uncles weren't looking as he licked the fizz off his hands and, without giving it much thought, took a good sip of beer. Inconspicuously he walked over to Tio Andres and gave him the opened bottle. Tio

Andres looked at him and then looked at the bottle. He made eye contact with Gabriel, indicating that he knew what had happened but he was going to let it slide.

Then Tio David said, "Hey kid, before you sit, get me a bottle."

Gabriel, feeling grown up, responded, "Sure thing!" and walked back to the cooler and popped open another bottle. He had enjoyed the first sip a bit more than he could have imagined so this time he decided to take a big gulp. By the time he put the bottle down, half the beer was gone. He tried to pretend like he had spilled it, "Oh! I can't believe it! I almost dropped the bottle! Sorry!" He walked over to Tio David and handed the bottle over.

Tio David looked at him, looked at the bottle, looked at Tio Andres, and then looked back at Gabriel one more time. "What's wrong with you kid? If you want a damn beer, get your own! Don't drink mine."

Gabriel's eyes widened, "For real! I can get one?"

Tio David laughed, "This kid is crazy, but yeah, go ahead finish this one and get me another one." Gabriel ran and handed Tio David another beer and the bottle opener. He sat on the towel next to them. They were carrying on and talking when Tio David took out a pack of cigarettes. The song, "Super Freak" came on. "This is one of Rick James' best songs!" he said as he got up and danced around. He looked like a chicken, flapping his arms as if they were wings, and lifted one leg at a time as if he had gas. It was the funniest dance Gabriel had ever seen. He bent over and cracked up. He laughed until tears streamed down his innocent face.

My uncles loved to party and Gabriel loved to watch how silly they were. Tio Andres turned the volume up as high as it could go, then looked at Tio David, "Hey brother give me a cigarette."

"Ok… Hey, Gabriel you want one?"

Gabriel thought he died and went to heaven. "Yes! I want one." My uncles started laughing.

Tio David looked at Tio Andres and said, "This kid is crazy! You're the best, Gabriel, never let anyone tell you otherwise but no, you can't have a cigarette! You want your mother to kill us?" They all laughed.

After about an hour Tio Andres said, "Alright, party's over. Let's get you back downstairs."

I had just gotten out of the shower and was about to go up to the roof when I heard them walking down the stairs. I noticed Gabriel wasn't feeling well. "Gabriel, what's wrong?"

He was laughing, "Nothing, mind your own bees wax! You're such a busy buddy!"

"You don't make sense, stupid!"

Tio Andres was about to say something to me, "Josefina…" and at that very moment, Mother walked in.

"Hi guys." They were all laughing and Tio Andres said, "Hey Beatrice, you're right – that couch looks good in the living room."

She walked past everyone and went into the living room. "It's better than an empty space and it looks fine here. Thanks!"

"Beatrice, we went up to the roof to listen to music and Gabriel drank a beer. He's fine."

Mother's expression changed, "That's not ok with me! Why did you allow him to do that?"

Tio David jumped in, "Oh man! Sorry sis. He's all right though, so no need to worry. Gabriel just wanted to be one of the guys. Don't get mad at him. It's not his fault."

Mother did not respond because she was too angry not to be rude. Instead, she nearly threw them out of the house. "Well, I'm going to clean the house a bit. I guess I'll see you guys at Mami's house?"

They got the point. "Alright sis, see you later. Oh yeah, and just relax please."

She never cracked a smile. After my uncles left the apartment, Mother called Gabriel into the living room and scolded him. "Gabriel, don't you ever let me hear that you drank alcohol again. I don't care if it's your uncle or your father or whomever – you never do that again. Do you understand?"

Gabriel thought Mother was overreacting but he knew better than to question her in that moment. He simply responded, "Yes Mom."

Mother was still angry, "Alcohol leads to other things! You're my son and you will be a healthy man. Your uncles think everything is a joke and I don't want you to think their behavior is normal!"

"May I be excused please?"

"Yes, you may."

I could hear him crying in his room. I felt bad for him but I knew Mother was right. Later I understood what Mother meant by, "I don't want you to think their behavior is normal." Tio Andres's story was not unique at the time but significant to our family. A short month after he migrated to New York from Colombia, the military police scooped him up off a corner and drafted him into the Army. He was not a United States citizen but it did not stop the military from deploying him to South Vietnam. He served three years before he returned to the States with a Purple Heart and post-traumatic stress disorder. Everyone respected his courage and dismissed the drug abuse problem he had inherited from his dark days in the war. Sometimes he would randomly talk about how he moved body parts to walk across the rivers and swamp areas in Vietnam. We'd all listen intently and beg for more details but he never indulged us.

Tio David was the youngest of mother's siblings. In the late 1970's he voluntarily enlisted in the military. He was a proud Marine who shared less traumatic stories about standing on deck with other Slimy Pollywogs and ceremonially getting hit with a paddle on the butt while the ship crossed the equator. The first time I remember seeing Tio David was about a year after we moved back to New York from Colombia. I was a young girl but I looked at my uncle and remember thinking he was so handsome dressed in his blue Marine uniform. His dirty blonde hair and gorgeous olive green colored, deep-set eyes sparkled and brightened his golden tan. His military high and tight recon cut sported his perfectly round head and accentuated his great facial features, especially his well-defined jaw line. He was tall at 6 feet 2 inches in height, and in amazing physical shape. It is probably inappropriate to admit he was my first crush, but I can say that he was a beautiful man and women loved him. He, however, was shy and probably never realized how attractive he really was. I loved when he'd call out "Oorah!" To have served the Marines was his pride and we all admired him for it. Whenever he was apart from Tio Andres he had a serious personality and was not very approachable, but together they were a trouble-making, fun duo. They were inseparable with a common love for drinking and telling stories, and this was why Mother frowned upon their casual attitude about drinking with Gabriel.

Later that day, Mother bought two twin-size wooden platform storage beds. She went to the local Woolworth store and purchased matching yellow bed sheets for my brother and me. The furniture was not pretty but we didn't care. I picked up a few posters of John Travolta and the Bee Gees at a dollar store to decorate my bedroom. My brother didn't care much for adorning his space so he opted to only have his bed and leave the open space in his small room. This did not matter because eventually we moved his bed into my room so we could play, talk, and watch TV together.

Gabriel was and is my best friend. I am glad our bond grew during this time and that we have always stayed close to one another. While we shared my room, we told jokes, listened to music, jumped on the giant homemade king size bed as if it was a trampoline... We had the most fun times!

We scared ourselves once by jumping so far up that it ricocheted Gabriel, slamming him against the vertical blinds. I had a vision flash before me of my brother smashing the glass and flying out the fifth floor window. I imagined the worst! I sighed deeply and let out an involuntary and disturbing sound. Everything happened so fast and I thought for certain he was hurt. The blinds tumbled down, landing on Gabriel's chest. He fell first on the edge of the bed and finally landed on the floor. Gabriel was in pain but I was relieved to see he had only suffered a small cut on his chest. After realizing he was fine, we laughed for hours. The games continued as if nothing had ever happened. For years we used our living room as an indoor playground, a roller-skating rink, a volleyball court, a dodge ball court. We even had fierce water balloon fights there.

A couple of days after Gabriel's fall, all was peaceful until the morning I woke up to a ruffling sound near the corner of my room. It was a bit startling so I sat up on my bed and rubbed my eyes in an effort to fully awaken. I squinted in the direction of where the disturbing squeaky sound was coming from. To my absolute terror I clearly got a glimpse of a mouse moving his tail near the clothes I had left on the floor. I screamed at the top of my lungs, waking Mother and Gabriel. Mother ran to my bedroom as I looked at her and said, "A mouse! Near my clothes!"

I found out that morning that Mother is terrified of mice. She said, "Josefina, hop over the bed and come out of the room." She couldn't find the courage to come in the room herself. In one leap I jumped into the living room, and Mother closed my bedroom door. She ran to the kitchen and phoned Tio Andres. "Andres, there's a mouse in Josefina's room, get over here as fast as you can!"

Tio Andres responded, "Calm down, it's not going to hurt you. Let me go to the bodega and get a trap and then I'll be on my way." Tio Andres had seen it all as a Vietnam veteran who was known in the neighborhood for being a tough guy. We were lucky to he lived a block away from us. We always felt protected since people in the neighborhood respected him and everyone knew he was our uncle. Mother, Gabriel and I went into Mother's room and locked the door. Mother was like a child. It was actually amusing to see she was just as scared as me. She would not allow Gabriel to go into my room and see if the mouse was still lingering in the same corner. Completely unable to help the situation, but in an effort to liven up the mood, she laughed and said, "Ok, so who' going to open the front door for Tio Andres when he gets here?"

I did not hesitate to respond, "Not me! So don't even think about asking me to do it."

She laughed and said, "Well! Lucky for us we have a man in the house. Gabriel, you'll be our savior today."

Gabriel looked at us both and said, "Not fair! I think I hate mice too, but I'm not sure."

Mother held his hand and said, "Gabriel, you don't hate mice, only Josefina and I do. You're the man of the house now."

He looked at Mother intensely and responded, "Ok." I chuckled at how easy it was to get Gabriel to do the dirty work.

We sat in Mother's room about twenty minutes. It seemed like an eternity as I anxiously peeked out the window and got a glimpse of Tio Andres. He had a brown paper bag in hand. "Mother, I can see Tio Andres! He's coming!"

Mother looked relieved, "Oh thank god! He took long enough. Gabriel, are you ready?"

As if being asked whether he was ready to jump out the window, Gabriel took a deep breath and responded, "Yes!" and in a very low tone he said, "I think." Tio Andres knocked on the door. Gabriel looked at Mother and me and, like a soldier going into a battle during a war, he opened the door just a tiny crack since Mother was afraid to open it wide enough to let the mouse in. Gabriel squeezed his skinny body out of the room, through the small opening and said, "I'm coming Tio Andres." Gabriel opened the door and, acting as if he had received a courage injection, he said, "Tio Andres, my mom and Josefina are panicked in Mom's bedroom."

Tio Andres smirked and then laughed. "Gabriel, women are afraid of nonsense. What the heck is a little mouse going to do to hurt you or anyone in the house? He's more afraid than they are." Gabriel stayed quiet because he did not want to lie about his fear of the mouse. On the way to Josefina's room, Tio Andres went into the kitchen and grabbed the broom. He continued, "Ok Gabriel, let's go into Josefina's room. You cover the door and make sure it doesn't get out."

Gabriel responded, "Ok, but what do I do if it comes near me?" Tio Andres seemed irritated, "You're kidding right? Huevon! You take the little critter and you pounce it with this broom!"

Gabriel did not have time to think about what Tio Andres had said. He grabbed the broom and responded, "You got it!"

Tio Andres knew Gabriel was scared but he was a no nonsense kind of man. He wasn't about to nurture a ridiculous fear, nor would he allow Gabriel to act like a scared girl. They walked into my room and closed the door tight. Tio Andres said, "Gabriel, I see him. He's kind of cute. He's terrified."

Gabriel couldn't help but feel sorry for him. "Well, if he's kind of cute, why are we hurting him?"

Tio Andres looked at him and asked, "Gabriel, you think your mother wants to live with a mouse?"

Gabriel felt sheepish and responded, "No sir!" Tio Andres, with a determined look, walked closer to the corner where the mouse stood petrified. He put his hand in the brown paper bag. He wanted to put the mouse in the bag so he could release it outside.

Gabriel held his breath as Tio Andres quietly walked to the corner. In a split second he bent down to grab the mouse when it scurried toward the bedroom door where Gabriel stood. Gabriel saw the little white creature as it came toward him and, without thinking of it

51

twice, gripped the broom stick tightly and, as if it was a hockey stick, swung with all his might. He somehow did the unimaginable. He had used enough force to trap the mouse against the broom's bristles and, like a hockey puck, the mouse went airborne right into the wall. Splat!

Tio Andres looked at Gabriel and started to laugh!

"That was great man! Good job!"

Gabriel felt proud and sad. He had handled the mouse like a man, but he couldn't help but think of how cute the little furry thing was. Of course, he would not divulge his feelings in front of the toughest guy in our family. He looked at Tio Andres and laughed, "That was a lucky shot."

Tio Andres wanted Gabriel to grow up a tough man. He felt Gabriel was at a disadvantage growing up in a house with only girls so he ignored Gabriel's obvious diminishing enthusiasm and gave him a high five. He then went on to put the dead mouse in the paper bag and told Gabriel, "Grab some detergent and clean up this area. I'm taking this thing to the dumpster." With the mouse in hand he walked quickly toward the front door while he said, "Ok, Beatrice, it's all clear. Bye!"

The next day Tio Andres brought us a stray kitten. He knocked on the door and I answered, "Hi Tio, how are you?" I noticed he had a backpack.

"I'm good. Where's your mother?"

I responded, "At work."

He proceeded to walk into the apartment and said, "I have a surprise for you guys."

I looked at him and said, "Really? I love surprises!"

He responded, "You're really going to love this one. All of you will."

"All of us? Should I call Gabriel over?"

"Yes! What the heck is he doing?"

"Gabriel! Tio Andres is here and he has a surprise for us!"

Gabriel was watching TV in the living room. I could hear his heavy walk toward the hallway. Tio Andres put his backpack down on the floor. He unbuckled the straps and out came the most beautiful kitten I had ever seen. My brother and I were thrilled to see the gorgeous, green eyed, gray and white, tiny beauty. She had a silky coat with a long, fluffy, luxurious looking tail. Mother agreed to keep her because she was terrified of mice and thought a cat would be a good way to keep mice out of our apartment.

We named the kitten Baby. Baby was playful and willful. She made it very difficult to get any sleep the first night she slept at our apartment. She purred loudly and kept jumping on and off my bed. I wanted to get some sleep so I placed her in the bathroom, figuring if she had to do her business it'd be best to have her in close proximity of the litter box but Baby had other plans. She tirelessly scratched at the bathroom door, and her persistent loud cries kept us up most of the night. I was convinced she would not settle for being alone so before sunrise I placed her back in my bed. Exhausted by Baby, I allowed her to lie on my chest, instantly falling prey to her irreplaceable company. Her rhythmic purring became a calming lullaby, her warmth a fuzzy blanket, and her companionship was a must from that day forward.

She seemed to be a perfect match for us. I carefully analyzed how she matured and felt sad that her playfulness only lasted a short year. She evolved into a snobbish fur ball that seemed annoyed by Gabriel and me. Her slow, classy walk and sexy look was the weapon she used to snub us, but while Baby was a kitten she took advantage of every opportunity to torture us. Her cue was our bare feet. She always attacked while we played dodge ball in the empty hallway that stretched from the front door to the living room. She would run as fast as she could and, with a swift jump, land on our feet, scratching us mercilessly. We would run away from her and she would chase us as if we were yarn balls. We took revenge by including her in our water balloon fights. She hated it and would escape at the sight of running water.

As a kitten she had enjoyed interrupting our games but as a grown cat she preferred watching television while purring on my chest. Her favorite shows seemed to be Tom & Jerry, Happy Days, Charlie's Angels, the Brady Bunch, and lots of soap operas. I still remember Baby, the intimidating, unapproachable cat who granted her affection exclusively to Gabriel and me, and whom we loved dearly.

Besides teasing Baby, Gabriel and I would spend time playing many other games. I still laugh when I think about how we pretended to be John Travolta and Olivia Newton John. We danced to the "Grease" soundtrack time after time. We danced a routine, which started with me as the lovely blonde, Sandy Olsson, wearing a yellow shawl on my head while I used candy cigarettes and pretended to smoke. My brother played a very cool Danny Zuko, but at times we'd switch roles. My brother would then wear the shawl and use the opportunity to poke fun at me. Luckily, the neighbors below us were three young guys who didn't mind the racket. They found it amusing and never complained about any of it.

All the while, Mother worked and went to college. Eventually, I became the substitute mother to Gabriel. I did everything; cooked, responded to any teacher concerns, checked our homework, fed Baby, and sometimes sang "Somewhere Over the Rainbow" for my brother before he'd fall asleep. We did not realize that a terrible burden had been placed on us. Gabriel and I were just one year apart in age but he needed more guidance than I did. By the time I turned ten and my brother nine, we were running the entire show in our home. Life had forced a heavy load on us and we had matured far beyond our years, although we still managed to put fun into our daily obligations.

Gabriel was always hungry… my solution was to open up a pancake business. I loved making pancakes, and my brother loved eating them. I charged him 5 cents a pancake. He'd always buy with the promise to pay me later, and he'd laugh because I was a terrible businessperson who never made a dime. I did the laundry and complained constantly about how unfair life had become. My brother, being the youngest, was assigned the job of errand boy. He spent half the day running back and forth between the grocery store and the apartment. Mother had made a deal with the owner of the grocery store who allowed us to buy groceries on a tab. My brother would sign all the receipts and my mother would stop at the grocery store every Saturday and pay the bill for the week's groceries. I don't know if my mother noticed that Gabriel was a terrible shopper. She was normally too tired to look at the receipts except for the one time Gabriel ran the bill up to over two hundred fifty dollars. She paid it and came home upset, not just because the bill was too high but because she had never seen so much junk purchased by anyone. I certainly enjoyed his choices enough not to say a word. He mainly purchased Bonkers, Kool-Aid, Chef Boyardee, Doritos, ice cream,

Yodels, and fake Victory candy cigarettes. I protected Gabriel by telling Mother, "Mom, we really missed having a warm meal." She felt so guilty that she calmed down and stopped scolding Gabriel and me. It was true that I envied the kids in our neighborhood that had packed lunches and evening dinners at their table, but we did not blame Mother. We loved her and knew she was doing her best.

Mother rewarded us every Sunday. She'd give us money to go to the movie theatre while she sat at the small kitchen table and studied. After the movies she'd have spaghetti ready for us to eat. I loved spaghetti. These were difficult but peaceful times.

CHAPTER 6

The day's heat refused to dissipate on a summer night in mid-June, 1981. There was no air-conditioning in our apartment so I strategically placed my bed flush against the wall and put a portable fan on a kitchen chair next to my bed. The dry, hot air circulated in my room, the invisible dust on the floor and furniture became airborne, dispersed, and accumulated on my sore throat, making it impossible to comfortably fall asleep. In a desperate attempt for relief, I drank a glass of cold water and pressed my body against the cool walls. It would only help for a brief while. Exhausted, irritated and covered in sweat, I tossed and turned until four in the morning. I woke up at 11:00 a.m. later that morning. After a near sleepless night I was grateful to be on summer break from school. I would have gladly wasted the day sleeping if it weren't for the excessive heat and the bedroom's disturbing bright white walls.

That morning I was perplexed and instantly irritated to hear my father's voice. Mother allowed him in earlier that morning. He arrived from Miami and Mami Abuela had taken him over to our apartment. Father had sporadically communicated with us via telephone but it was awkward to see him on this first visit to New York. Mami Abuela had an old fashioned mindset. She indisputably believed a woman's place was with her husband. That summer morning she acted in good faith and had the best intentions at heart. She knew our struggles and thought our father could make it better for us. Mother confided later that she felt stunned at the sight of Father when she answered the knock on the door. The surprise disabled her and, without any protest, she allowed Father inside the apartment.

I was an 11-year-old kid who had missed him so much, but the thought that he did not love us angered me. I felt a rush of mixed feelings after hearing his voice. I wondered why he had come to our house and why Mother allowed him into our new life after everything that had happened.

There he was standing in front of me. I tried to contain the excitement at seeing him again. He said, "Hello Josefina! Come here my beautiful girl."

I expected a reaction from Mother. I thought she would confront him about his abandonment but she said and did nothing. She acted as if he had never failed any of us. She was defenseless and I was a well-mannered girl. Mother had taught us to love him despite his shortcomings. I responded "Hi Papi," and walked over to offer him a polite greeting. Instead, a burst of tears silently wet his shirt as he hugged me tightly. I was terrified to admit that deep inside I was glad to see him, that he made me feel secure and protected, that I wanted him to stay and help Mother, that I still saw him with the same loving eyes with which a little girl sees her dad.

Sadly, his two-day stay marked a new established pattern. He entered and left our lives at will. I was young and found Father's pit stop a disappointment, an annoyance, and well-defined disrespect. Mother, on the other hand, lived a bewildered existence and was incapable of standing up for herself. She was blinded by a repressed upbringing and could not predict the terrible repercussions her tolerance would have on our lives. The undoubtedly significant negative psychological consequences on Mother, Gabriel and me would be evident for decades to come. Mother, a decent woman who truly lived by example, raised us as best she could but failed to see that she had instilled a contradictory belief system in our home. On the one hand, she was strong and taught us the value of hard work in order to achieve personal goals. On the other, she struggled with her self-esteem and continuously allowed Father to undermine her personal accomplishments and diminish her self-worth.

I was just an innocent kid, unable to process any of it. Instead, I accepted the rhythm and patterns in our lives. After Father's visits, we simply returned to Mother's well-known routine. We worked hard together, we were grateful for what we had, and we loved and protected one another every day.

During the summers Gabriel and I typically kept all the windows open. We would go out the second bedroom window and onto a horizontal platform protected by railings. The fire escape was a favored place where we hoped to capture a hint of breeze in the overwhelmingly stagnant heat. Mother had strict rules about street safety. She allowed us to use the apartment as an indoor playground but we had to wait until she was home from work before we could play outside with the rest of the neighborhood kids.

During her working hours we watched the action from our bedroom window or on the fire escape. Sol, our next-door neighbor, would do the same. To escape the apartment's heat, Gabriel, Sol, and I talked and played on the fire escape almost all night. We had a great view of all the kids roller-skating, playing handball and two-handed touch football on the paved streets of Washington Heights. We couldn't wait for the weekends. Mother would take us downstairs and allowed us to join in the fun. She did not entirely approve of the people in the neighborhood because she believed we were special and did not want us having friendships with just anyone. She wanted us to be selective and to stay away from the known troublemakers, and we did. On hotter days it was almost a certainty that someone would find a way to illegally turn open the valve of the fire hydrant. Water would pour onto the sidewalk and flow forcefully onto the street. We, the neighborhood kids, would ecstatically get soaked in the powerful stream of freezing cold water. It was better than a swimming pool because we could also drink it if we became thirsty from playing in the sun. It was the happiest time for Gabriel and I, and we laughed at how silly we all looked while splashing water on each other. Part of the fun for the neighborhood kids was running away from the cops when they arrived to shut off the hydrant.

Summers were awesome. I especially enjoyed the weekend plans with our extended family, particularly spending time with mother's cousin, Ned, who was like an uncle to us. He was always with his girlfriend, Zora, and his best friend whom we called Uncle Will. Uncle Will was an Irish man whose family lived in California and adopted us as his surrogate family. Together we enjoyed many fun road trips. Tio Ned favored driving the scenic mountainous roads southwest of the city of Syracuse to Otisco Lake. It was his favorite of the Finger Lakes in upstate New York. The road trips gave all of us an opportunity to enjoy nature without the obstruction of the big city buildings. Another preferred destination was Bear Mountain State Park where I had hoped to get a glance of the famous Black Bear. Luckily I had been spared the excitement as we freely walked around the park, had picnics, played Frisbee, enjoyed a game of two-handed touch football, and drove home.

I will always cherish the time we visited Perkins Memorial Drive and Tower. The climate was perfect that day. The clear, true-blue colored sky was uplifting. A cool wind brushed softly against my face as I marveled over the spectacular view of the lush, green park, the peaks of the Catskill Mountains, and I even got a glance of the skyline formed by New York City skyscrapers. I fantasized about being Rapunzel and wished I had long, braided hair to swing down from the window at the top of the tower. I did not expect a prince to climb up; I thought it would be a delightful way for everyone on the ground to come up and join the enchanted fantasy inspired by this captivating place.

Mother's family did many things together. The big group consisted of grandparents, uncles, aunts, cousins, and friends. Apart from Tia Ana, who always seemed disturbed, I enjoyed everyone's company. In the summers we loved going to Orchard Beach in the Bronx. Everyone laughed at how dirty the water was but no one seemed to really care. It was so murky that we nicknamed it "la playa de los mojones." It wasn't unusual to see a chicken bone or a shoe floating on the surface. We never thought anything of it; as far as we were concerned it was all part of the fun. Sometimes we would go to Jones Beach, which was much nicer but very far from Washington Heights.

To get the most out of the trip we'd spend the entire day at the beach. Mother never paid attention to the importance of sunscreen so Gabriel and I would be exposed to the sun all day without any protection and we suffered the most terrible sunburns. Worse yet, on this one occasion I became so dehydrated that I passed out on the beach. I was unresponsive so the local authorities were called. An ambulance drove onto the sand where I lay unconscious. The emergency medical technician considered my state life threatening so a helicopter was called on the scene. I was taken by helicopter to the local hospital where I was given intravenous rehydration. Once my fluids were replaced I felt the strength to say, "I hope we can still go to the beach next weekend." Everyone felt relieved when I showed a sign that I had fully recovered and was only sorry that I could not recall the helicopter ride. I thought, "What a waste of a great trip!"

The 1981 Fourth of July fireworks celebrations were accompanied by rain that began early morning and lasted for much of the day. The rain-soaked streets were gloomy, and Gabriel and I were upset until Tio Ned and Uncle Will showed up. They brought their cars to drive the family members who were interested in watching the fireworks. Uncle Will was on duty. He was to follow Tio Ned's car, which was no easy task. I love Tio Ned but he was by far the worst driver on the planet. Given that the weather at that year's Fourth of July celebration were expected to be especially hectic combined with Tio Ned's driving, it was to be nothing short of frightening.

Uncle Will always joined the family to watch the fireworks. That year to ensure he would not lose Tio Ned's car in the chaotic New York City traffic, he came up with several plans which were designed to reinforce the many original plans we had for that night. Uncle Will took into consideration weather, crowds, crime, parking spaces, and so on. He called in a plan A, and if that failed, we were instructed to follow a plan B and, worst-case scenario, we were to go on to plan C. We laughed at his enthusiasm and enjoyed every minute of his company. Luckily the rain stopped during the prime fireworks time and, thanks to Uncle Will's amazing ability to follow Tio Ned's car, we were able to watch the spectacle all together.

Tio Ned and his friends helped create many memorable fun times for us. Although Uncle Will never seemed awkward around Tio Ned and his girlfriend, I sometimes suspected he was secretly in love with Zora. I thought he liked being around us for an opportunity to be near her. Mother's response to my suspicions was, "Josefina stop watching soaps. It's filling your head with absolute nonsense! Besides, don't you have some kid stuff to worry about?" I was a curious girl and kept my eyes open. Fortunately there was never any clear indication to confirm my suspicions, so the possibility remained a dramatic entertainment for me. Truthfully, we all had such a great time together that his motives really did not matter at all. As I matured I understood we were his family and he was a real uncle to Gabriel and me.

Among the most impressive experiences was when they took Gabriel and me to our first Yankee's game at Yankee Stadium in the Bronx. I vividly remember the first time I looked at the enormous stadium with its beautiful green diamond surrounded by the deep red color dirt and the green grass in the outfield. It was an exhilarating experience similar to the one I experienced the first time I visited Disney and saw Mickey Mouse. The stadium was nicknamed "The House That Ruth Built" after the legendary Babe Ruth. I was in awe of the grand stadium. I blissfully walked down the cement steps and strolled into the aisle, kicked a bunch of empty peanut shells out of the way, and sat on the blue stadium seat. I thought of the numerous major league baseball players that had contributed to the exceptional baseball played on that field. The brilliant colors on the field accentuated the logo with the proudly displayed NY letters near the home plate. Along the side I could see the enormous blue colored team name Yankee. Everything that day seemed magical! The smell of popcorn and the vendors walking around the stadium calling out loudly, "Hotdogs here! Hamburgers! Peanuts! Ice cold drinks!" What a day! I was a kid from Colombia who loved this land more than any other place on God's green earth. That day I lived an unforgettable, most remarkable American dream.

Everything was normal, nice, comfortable, and sometimes amazing. One day Mother received a phone call from Tia Matilde. She told her Magdalena missed us and wanted to visit New York for a week. She asked if it was OK for her to stay at our house. Mother, of course, agreed and thought it would be terrific. Mother was pleased about Magdalena visiting because she knew it would make me very happy.

Two weeks later Magdalena arrived. I could barely contain my excitement when I saw her walking out of the Customs terminal. She looked radiant. I could see she had not changed at all. I could see her cheerful smile, sparkling white beautiful teeth, and striking, sweet, caramel colored eyes that melted the heart of anyone who dared glance at her even from a mile away. A rush of excitement came over me and without giving it much thought, I ran past the security point to greet her. I was called back by an airport guard, prompting Magdalena to speed walk toward me. We hugged tightly. I could smell her fragrance with a mixture of minty gum and new leather that permeated from her large purse. She tried to lift me as if I was still a small child, but failed. "Josefina! You look so grown up! Beautiful girl, I've missed you!" I looked at her as tears ran down my face. I was so happy I actually cried. In my heart Magdalena was my big sister. I felt nostalgic at the sight of her. It reminded me of sad and happy times in Colombia. She looked at me and wiped the tears off my face. "Oh, silly girl! No crying! Let's have some fun!"

I could not think of anything that could possibly make this summer any better. Mother drove while Magdalena reminded us of old stories from when we lived in Colombia and shared that she was engaged to a wonderful man and that she wished we could go to her wedding. "Josefina, Tia Matilde missed all of you dearly, but she's very happy that you've establish a new life here." She went on to talk about her studies and her work. I admired how she seemed to consider herself very fortunate and never took any of her blessings for granted.

Mother parked the car in front of our apartment building and, for a split second, I felt a bit embarrassed. Magdalena lived in a lovely home and our apartment was, simply put, plain poor. Then I remembered that Magdalena was far from pretentious. She was kind and nonjudgmental.

Mother and Magdalena carried the luggage up the five flights. We spent the night catching up and I volunteered to be her tourist guide.

During the next few days we enjoyed New York the way tourists do. My favorite was the first attraction we visited: The American Museum of Natural History. I'll always remember sitting in the Hayden Sphere. The Planetarium was an enchanting place for me. I felt thrilled to learn about the wonders of our universe and fascinated by the knowledge that our sun is only one among millions of stars.

The next day we visited the Empire State Building and enjoyed a magnificent view of the New York/New Jersey area. We did so much that week, and even took a sightseeing cruise around the island of Manhattan aboard the Circle Line. We traveled south on the Hudson River to the southern tip of Manhattan where we saw the Statue of Liberty and the awe-inspiring Verrazano Bridge. The boat proceeded through the upper bay and headed north up the East River to the Harlem River. Along the way we enjoyed a glimpse of the five boroughs. I'll never forget the sight of the legendary places we saw along the way; Ellis Island, Yankee Stadium, and the unique greenery in Inwood Hill Park along the northern tip of Manhattan leading back into the Hudson River. The swift sail under the incomparable George Washington Bridge was frightening and delightful. I will always remember cousin Magdalena's visit to New York as the one of the most special memories of my youth.

By this time I considered myself a prototypical New Yorker who was always rushed and commonly failed to see the real beauty of the city. Magdalena's visit was magical. I was able to see and photograph so many of the iconic places that give the city its allure. The experience truly awakened the passion I felt for the city I loved.

The day before Magdalena was to return to Colombia, I accompanied her while she shopped for gifts for her mom and dad. Mother suggested we go to Macy's on 34th street in mid-town. Magdalena asked if I minded making a quick stop at Saint Patrick's Cathedral. I was so happy at the suggestion. I loved the church, and Saint Patricks' impressive history and amazing architecture made it a terrific place to visit. We took a city bus down Madison Avenue to the front of the Cathedral. We quietly walked inside and proceeded down the aisle to the front altar. There we kneeled and Magdalena whispered to me, "Josefina, say a prayer for our family. I will give thanks to God for this beautiful visit and for your wonderful company." I looked at her and held her hand. She had been a big sister, someone I could trust, and someone I would love forever. I hated the thought that her visit was near its end.

The following morning we drove Magdalena to the airport. I cried almost the whole way there while she tried to console me, saying, "Josefina, I'll come visit again. Maybe you can visit me in Colombia. I wish you could go to my wedding!" I knew that would not be possible since mother held a deep resentment toward Colombia, but I appreciated her kind invitation. She noticed that missing her wedding really upset me and did the best she could to comfort me. "Don't worry, I'm sure we'll be together in spirit. As soon as I get pictures of the wedding, I will send them to you."

We parked the car at the airport and waited while she boarded the plane. As I watch her flight lift off the runway, a deep nostalgic feeling overtook me. I yearned to be in her company again. I should have felt happy about our time together, but instead I was consumed with an inexplicable sadness. Later that night I cried myself to sleep. I missed Magdalena so much. We had fallen back into our big sister, little sister routine. Neither one of us had a sister to share secrets, dreams, and fears with. For a brief moment we enjoyed a true sisterhood.

Back then, calling Colombia was so expensive that it was only done for emergencies. We both promised to write one another often and for a while we did. Then reality set in, with all the distractions in our daily, busy schedules. We would send each other the occasional letter, but eventually our busy lives would distract us without time to write to each other. Time and distance would drift us apart again.

As close as I was to Gabriel, I couldn't tell him girl secrets; he would just make fun of me. Mother said, "Josefina, stop being silly and be happy about the time you spent with Magdalena. Stop acting like you're never going to see her again and get some sleep." Mother had a way of dealing with my drama that was borderline cold. I felt I had no option but to simply go to sleep.

CHAPTER 7

Just when things fell into a routine, Father would find a way to disrupt the peace. He phoned Mother on December 23rd, 1982 and I could hear his voice come through the phone.

Father said, "I need you and the kids to pick me up at the airport. My flight arrives at 6:00 p.m."

Mother responded, "Tonight?"

Father, "Yes, I have to go because I've got to get ready my flight. See you all soon."

Mother hung up the phone, and with an excited voice called out to Gabriel and I, "Josefina, Gabriel, your dad just phoned. He's getting in tonight and wants to spend Christmas with us. Let's hurry up and get the house organized." I wanted to roll my eyes but would never dare disrespect Mother. We hurriedly picked up the house, mopped the floors, wiped the furniture clean, turned on the Christmas tree lights, and headed to the airport. We arrived at the airport at about 5:45 p.m., parked the car in the short-term lot and walked to the terminal. Gabriel and I were playing around and joking as we waited for the passengers on the Miami flight to deplane. We anxiously expected Father to walk out but as the crew disembarked it became obvious that the last passengers on the flight had already walked out into the terminal. We were confused and thought perhaps he had missed the flight. Mother phoned him from a public phone booth but he did not pick up his house phone. She phoned him again. She was afraid to leave the airport. I can still hear her say, "Josefina,

Gabriel, just sit and wait. He's probably on another flight. I might have written the information down wrong. Stop pestering me, be patient please."

We waited for over thirty minutes before she finally decided it was time for us to leave the airport. It was a very quiet car ride home. That night the airport seemed far from Manhattan. It was illogical to think he had missed the flight and did not bother to inform us to at least spare us the unnecessary road trip to the airport. We silently dragged our legs up the five flights to our apartment. Mother finally said, "If he's busy that's fine. It'll give us an opportunity to enjoy Christmas our way. Josefina, I know you like it when it's just us." Gabriel and I did not respond.

We walked into the apartment and Mother walked straight to our house phone and called him again. He did not pick up. At this point, even I was worried something had happened. After a half hour she finally received a phone call from him.

Father said, "Hey, I am sorry I missed the flight. I couldn't get to a phone until now but I will see if I can make it to New York before the end of the year. I'll call you and let you know."

Mother responded, "We were at the airport. The kids and I were worried."

Father made no excuses and his apology seemed insincere and unacceptable to me. "Tell them I'll try to see them before the end of the year. Let them know I could not get to the plane on time." Before she could say anything else, he said, "I have to go, I'm in the middle of an important meeting," and hung up.

I grabbed the phone and called his house. Surprisingly, he answered. "Father, don't ever come back here. You are not welcome in our home anymore." Before he could respond, I hung up on him. Gabriel became very upset with me. He cried as he said, "Josefina! Why did you do that? Now he's never going to want to come see us again!" I was furious and did not regret calling Father but I felt bad for Gabriel and Mother. I apologized and went to my room. I cried loudly while tears streamed down my face, feeling sorry for Mother, Gabriel, and myself. I did not want them to be angry with me. My pillow was soaked in a puddle of tears, so I turned it to find a dry spot. I rested my head on the dry side and was about to fall asleep, feeling stressed from the unpleasantness of the incident when Mother walked in my room and hugged me. I've never seen her so angry. It was acceptable for Father to hurt her but when he disappointed us it was deeply painful. She did not say much to avoid adding more negativity to my feelings, but instead she got in bed with me, cuddled me, and allowed me to fall asleep in her arms.

The next day we did not discuss what had happened. Once again, everything was swept under the rug. There would be no mention from my parents on how to repair the reoccurring disappointments. Instead, Father continued to visit whenever he pleased. There were no prearranged agreements made. He arbitrarily visited and stayed at will, and he always took over the role of head of the house, destabilizing any progress we had made to live normal lives.

I was getting older and things were not adding up for me. I began to question the unusual circumstances. I was aggravated by the inconsistency and had difficulty forgiving Mother for allowing him back into our lives time and time again. I imagined a world where she would have the courage to not open the door, a world where she would get rid of him and never allow him to hurt her again.

By my thirteenth birthday the paradox was evident to me. Clearly my mother, my superhero, a strong and proud woman capable of starting a new life in a new country, was debilitated by a hereditary glitch.

She was a fearless worker, educating herself in hopes of a brighter future, yet paralyzed by a mindset that demanded a woman's loyalty be first and foremost to her husband. Mother was handicapped by a mentality that overpowered a woman's own sense of survival and allowed the acceptance of unacceptable men. In our case, this was not just any man, it was our father who used our house like a revolving door, a temporary shelter. His reentering our lives was disturbing and absurd. Mother sacrificed herself, her self-respect, and us. The thought was sickening and at times traumatizing.

We had witnessed multiple incidences of disrespect, yet Mother demanded we respect him. Although she had lived an ethical life herself, she permitted this man to taint and darken her and all that surrounded her. As I continued to mature I wondered if she had ever learned any rules other than the ones instilled on her. No! Her rules were not defined as black or white. I realized her upbringing was a murky gray area. I was marveled by her strength and perplexed by her foolishness. Was it possible that Mami Abuela's ruling thumb, in fact, imposed our father on us? Could this be possible or did Mother willingly allow him to stay and use excuses to disguise her overpowering weakness as it related to Father? We lived in what I would often call a gray area. Our mother called it "her upbringing". Either way, it was terrible.

My brother and I lived confused and were rendered powerless by Father's dominance on our mother. Our family lived in a perpetual gray area, which, by definition, is an ill-defined situation or field not readily conforming to a category or to an existing set of rules. They did not live together full-time, they were not officially separated, and they would not file for divorce. It was all very confusing.

Mother, my superhero, had lost all strength. The gray area was where opposites inexplicably coexisted. Shame reigned easily, accompanied by love and pride. It was where her vulnerability was exposed and her shining spirit was dulled.

I woke up early one morning during one of Father's visits. Feeling hungry, I headed toward the kitchen. As I glanced over to Mother's room, I noticed Father was not there. I heard the shower running and I don't know why, but I decided to walk into the bedroom. I saw his suitcase lying on the floor, open. I really did not intend on snooping around, but I walked in past the suitcase and noticed what seemed like an empty leather briefcase by the bedside.

Almost instinctively I looked at the mirror by the closet. I didn't like to fuss over my hair. It was cut very short to stop an old habit I had of twirling my hair and putting it in my mouth while I slept; a habit that my brother teased me about, a habit my mother scolded me over. As I looked at myself in the mirror, I could hear my mother say, "You and your knots, and the stinking slobbering all over the pillow! Your hair will stay short until you stop that nasty habit. You're ruining your beautiful hair!" At the time I still considered myself somewhat of a tomboy. The haircut did not bother me but the hair sticking out in complete disarray was distracting. I walked past the mirror and noticed the closet door was slightly open so I peaked in. There were no rules about privacy in our house. Drawers were opened and closed without restrictions; there had never been a single warning about not entering Mother's room and looking through stuff. But even if there had been, it would not have applied. What I saw was in plain view. It was displayed for the amusement of all those curious kids who were interested in taking a quick peek. My innocence was not so innocent and I knew exactly what was staring at me. I was stunned and afraid. Was this white powdery substance for my father's use?

I quickly left the bedroom, knowing exactly what I had just seen, knowing it was not a good thing, wondering if that was the reason my dad appeared to be unemployed, wondering if he was an addict. Was he...? The thought of what I had seen stayed in my mind for the rest of the day. I couldn't wait for Mother to get home from work. I needed answers. Our mother had created an open relationship with us and allowed us to speak our minds. She respected our thoughts and encouraged honesty, so I was not afraid to confront her.

That evening I could barely wait to question Mother. As soon as she walked through the door I said, "Mother, I need to speak to you, it's important."

As she removed her coat she responded, "What's wrong Josefina?"

"Mom, I saw the bag in your closet. It had a white powder in it. It looked like a bag of cocaine in your closet. I know that's not yours. Is Dad using drugs?"

An otherwise expressionless woman was obviously shocked and dumbfounded by my honesty. She recovered quickly, "Cocaine? What do you know about drugs?"

At that moment I realized I was unprepared, yet forced into having an adult conversation with Mother. I responded, "I don't know anything about drugs."

"NO! He doesn't use that stuff. I can't control what your father does, and I really don't know why he has that garbage." Her aloof reaction wasn't as surprising as it should have been. She never had the courage to deal with the reality as it pertained to father. I continued to question her and she finally responded. "He said he doesn't sell it, but I don't know."

I was an astute and observant young girl and began analyzing the facts. It all started to make sense. He lived in Miami but travelled frequently to Colombia and New York. He never kept a real schedule or followed any patterns. In the past I had asked myself, "Shouldn't father be at work somewhere like all of my friend's dads?" I had heard many derogatory comments about Colombians being drug dealers. I hated that there was a possibility we fit the negative stereotype. The popular belief that all Colombians were drug dealers was a sore subject since many people around us openly voiced that assumption.

Ironically, in a disturbing way, I felt relieved. I finally understood why certain things were happening in our home. While we lived in Colombia, Father had an office but he was rarely ever there. He traveled often and always had stacks of cash. Whenever he visited New York, he seemed to be doing well financially but he lacked structure and discipline so he only contributed to our needs when he was around. Mother had to work long, hard hours for us to barely get by while he disregarded us in a reproachable manner.

The discovery of drugs in Mother's bedroom happened simultaneously with President Reagan's wife, First Lady Nancy Reagan's, very public "Just Say No" anti-drug campaign. Ironically, this campaign aligned with Mother's beliefs and teachings about drugs and resisting peer pressure. Children in public schools were taught to stay away from the recreational use of drugs, violence and premarital sex. The anti-drug movement was partially adopted by the Catholic school system and integrated slowly, with a religious twist. Students in our school were sheltered and not given the same anti-drug exposure. Our school focused mainly on God's love and his purpose for us, which I believe was instrumental in keeping Gabriel and I away from many potentially devastating social influences. Our school was not explicit about the terrible impact such dealings had on society as a whole, but fortunately Mother did teach us about resisting peer pressure and not being followers. She'd often say,

"Don't be sheep! It erases you as a person and it disappoints God… More importantly, if anyone offers you a taste of

junk, don't be afraid to turn away from that person." I knew what she meant when she used the term 'junk' but I had been oblivious that Father, a man I couldn't help but love, a man I was supposed to respect, was contributing to a widespread disease that afflicted so many people, particularly in the 80's and 90's.

At the time of my discovery, I really was not concerned with Father's dealings because I did not fully grasp the reality of the whole situation. In the beginning it was over my head, but it all slowly began to add up as I got older and started to think suspiciously about certain past experiences. I had a flashback to customs at the Miami Airport when we first arrived from Colombia. I didn't understand mother's nervousness and the puzzling fear about standing too close to a stranger. I didn't know why this impacted my eight-year-old brain, but it did. I was just a kid but couldn't ignore Mother's emphatic disconnect from the stranger, whom she had talked to during most of the two and a half hour flight. I had always questioned why she had been slightly rude to the nice stranger but could not figure it out until now. She knew the kind of business that could put people in jail for a long time. She feared many people from Colombia were involved in such dealings and wanted no part of it, yet she was married to a man who was involved in things she had taken a definite stand against. I had unwillingly seen a glimpse of Father's business dealings and Mother's contradictions. It was all too confusing for my young years.

CHAPTER 8

For a couple of years Father's life was indirectly related to us. His pattern of appearing and disappearing, in and out of our lives, had become the norm. I didn't give the white powder in the closet incident much thought after that, and Father's business was not discussed for many years to come. We ignored all the irritating things that connected us to our father, like the fact that he never really paid child support or contributed to our home's expenses unless he was staying with us at the apartment. We lived financially stricken until he visited. My father lived a different life than we did, and he shared his lifestyle with us during his short, intermittent visits. When he was around, it was like Christmas. He rewarded Gabriel and me for our good grades and the hard work we did to help around the house. He would take us to Saks Fifth Avenue on shopping sprees. He'd buy clothes, sweaters, coats, gloves, socks, shoes… anything we needed and wanted. Mother was frugal to a fault and hated his so-called "waste of money". I would feel upset with her for not allowing us to indulge in his sporadic generosity.

Mother was determined to save money because she earned it honestly. She worked many hours and understood the value of a dollar. She was always busy and focused on our savings so intensely that she was continuously unaware of important details. One of her greatest weaknesses was that she often neglected to notice that spending money was sometimes a matter of requirement. I wore an old pair of black and white skippy shoes throughout the year's seasons. In the dead of winter I wore a coat that was coming apart at the seams and had holes in the pockets. Experiencing the indescribable pain of nearly frostbitten toes and the uncontrollable shivers due to being chilled to the bone during snowstorms was life altering. I probably would have preferred a pair of boots and a real coat to a favorite meal. I dreamed of an easier life but never complained. I understood it was part of the necessary struggles and I didn't want to disturb Mother's plan.

I was grateful Father was different. He gave us a break from the regimen and the poverty. There were many things about him that I really cherished and loved. He was affectionate, playful, funny, and liked spoiling Gabriel and I. He did not follow a schedule and preferred to eat late at night. While Gabriel and I struggled to fall asleep on a school night, he would find a way to entertain us. It would always start with the loud sound of the blender turned on in the kitchen. We knew exactly when he was about to sneak into our room, so we'd pretend to be asleep while he held a tray with either watermelon shakes or chocolate milkshakes and buttered toast. He'd walk in the bedroom and clear his throat, sigh, and say out loud, "Oh well, they've fallen asleep. I guess I'll have to drink these shakes by myself..."

We would jump up laughing, "No! No! We're awake, Papi!" I really looked forward to the delicious, icy chocolate shakes. The watermelon was really good too but what I appreciated most was the temporary relaxed environment. When he was around I could be a kid without obligations. He allowed us to watch TV while we slowly sipped the shakes to take advantage of breaking our curfew. Sometimes we would start playing games. We'd jump on our bed or Father would allow us to go to the living room and watch either Hulk Hogan wrestling, Star Trek, or Bruce Lee movies on TV.

Mother would always protest, "Go to bed! You need to get up early for school! Octavio, you'll have to deal with them when they refuse to get up for school in the morning." He'd always laugh and accuse us of getting him into trouble.

Father's great sense of humor was polar opposite to Mother's attitude. We seldom noticed him upset. He was upbeat and very likable, and would talk about how he and his friends played dominos in "El Paseo de Bolivar" near La Iglesia de San Nicolas de Tolentino in Barranquilla. He would joke, using slang about eating butifarras with bollo, and we would laugh out loud although we had heard the same jokes hundreds of times before. Whenever our friends came to the apartment to hang out, we would play The Sugarhill Gang records and Father would come into the room and pretend to be a Rapper. It was very comical. He'd play Planet Patrol's "Play At Your Own Risk" and automatically go into the glide master or a flip rock, followed by a kid nice and he'd finish with an icy ice. He was not afraid to hit the floor! All my friends celebrated his Breakdance moves "Go Mr. L! Go!" since they couldn't pronounce Octavio, while I covered my face pretending to be embarrassed.

Father was handsome and charming. I still hear his melodic voice singing while he showered. He would always bathe in John Maria Farina cologne so the scent permeated through the walls, bringing abundance into the otherwise modest apartment. The cologne smelled clean, soft and elegant, in perfect synchrony with his persona. He was always well groomed and looked classy, even when he dressed in a casual white t-shirt and a pair of blue jeans. Generally, he had good fashion sense and stylishly sported wide collar shirts with loose-bottom trousers. He and Mother looked good together. I loved the pair of royal blue denim overalls she wore with a ladies Kangol black hat. Around him she looked stress-free, lovely, and had a bright smile.

Father learned English at the American School in Bogota, Colombia. He spoke an eloquent, sort of distinguished British English and could fit in any social setting. Going out to dinner with my father was eventful. He loved taking us to fancy restaurants. We'd dress in our best clothes and drive south to Lower Manhattan. I remember my favorite all black outfit: a shoulder-less, long sleeve top with a miniskirt, leggings, and ankle boots. I did not care to accessorize much so I would complete the look by simply wearing some lip-gloss. The warmest memory of such outings was the day Father took us to what was considered to be one of the most exclusive dining places at the time.

Windows on the World restaurant was located on the top 106th and 107th floors of the North Tower of the World Trade Center. The view of Manhattan's skyline was astounding. I vividly remember silently staring out the panoramic windows in reverence of the building's massiveness. It was an absolutely breathtaking marvel. Dining at Window on the World was similar to dreaming for me, being able to enjoy the extraordinary view of Manhattan's southern tip where the Hudson and the East River meet. To the east there were the bridges of Brooklyn, Queens, and Staten Island, and to the west a peak at parts of New Jersey. Throughout the skies, I got to enjoy the spectacle of airplanes arriving and departing from the New York / New Jersey airports. This place simultaneously represented the grandeur of human possibility and the miniaturization of everything. I recall mixing with the upper class, and the exquisite tasting food was genuinely a rare delight for my brother, mother, and me. I felt grown up standing by the bar area with a Coca Cola in hand, waiting for a table. The men were required to wear a sports jacket and the women were attractive, classy, enviable... The formal attire added a flare of refinement and snootiness to the place, which I felt enigmatically drawn to.

I had a vague recollection of how, before our travels to Colombia, Father had taken us to a construction site. He mentioned he and Mother had marveled over the deep hole that would house the architectural giant. He said, "The dirt excavated alone will expand the Manhattan shoreline across West Street and they will use the new land to build a place they will call Battery Park City. Brilliant engineering!"

Father shared wonderful moments with us, always predictably followed by his departure. Mother was stuck in a life without definition. Her relationship with Father was toxic, like lead poisoning affecting brain function. It was as if she had a serious neuropsychological problem that debilitated and destroyed her ability to choose and fulfill any of her own personal dreams.

My parents got along great during his stays, better than they ever had while they lived together. Mother seemed fulfilled by his periodic visits. I determined from my personal observations that for a long time she was stuck in limbo, unable to leave an old love or desire a new love, unable to abandon the past, the tired rut, and start a fresh, unspoiled adventure. When she boarded the plane in Barranquilla, I believed it was in search of a new beginning; I came to understand she simply transferred locations, with her life remaining the same. She spent most of her time working, studying, and waiting for Father to decide when he would visit again.

Gabriel and I inevitably grew resentful of her deep depression and her mental absence from our lives. In her darkest moment she spent four days in bed. Gabriel and I were worried and alone. We phoned Mother's brother, Tio David, who kindly came to our home and cooked us dinner. He made a "levanta muerto" soup for Mother and assured us she would be fine. I've always loved Tio David for his extreme kindness. That day he was a true lifesaver. I believe it was his soup that kicked-started Mother's recovery.

Gabriel and I questioned where Father was during these trying moments. I missed his presence and felt overwhelmed, as if I was the parent and Mother was an insecure child. I began to question where Father was on a winter Sunday when a town hoodlum punched my brother in the face at the front of our local church. My defenseless brother felt afraid and Mother was incapable of protecting him. I instinctively got involved in the middle of the commotion and pushed my brother's attacker. Luckily, some of the people coming out of church noticed and helped avoid any further physical confrontations. Once again, the aftermaths of confronting a bully was insufferable. The neighborhood kids joked about me openly. They nicknamed me "Rocky" after the famous movie character, Rocky Balboa. Every time I walked around the neighborhood, kids would tease me. They would sing Rocky's theme song, "Gonna Fly Now," and they'd loudly call out "Go, Rocky go!" I hated it! Despite the ridicule and the embarrassment, sticking up for my brother was my duty. If I had to do it again, I would.

Getting over being teased by the neighborhood kids was the least of my problems. There were many growing pains in a neighborhood that was undoubtedly deteriorating. The most significant was the day a sick rapist almost made my classmates and me his victim. I still vividly recall that traumatic day. I had entered the building where I lived, along with two school friends, during our lunch break. The building had an intercom system, so it required someone trying to enter to either phone a tenant who would buzz them in or, if you were a resident, input a numeric code which opened the door. A well-dressed young man wearing a liberal amount of cologne followed us inside. Ironically, I punched in the code and held the door open for the intruder, thereby bypassing the only security method. We all walked up the stairwell between the second and third floors when the stranger abruptly stopped. He stood in the middle and kept us from moving forward. He pulled down his zipper and took out his private part and demanded we follow him to the roof. He claimed to have a gun in his pocket and proceeded to threaten us. He stated that if we didn't do what he commanded, he would not hesitate to kill us. I can't remember much else he said beyond that point. I was so terrified that I blanked out for a brief moment. Only my guardian angel could have protected me at this point. In a foggy state, I recall submissively following him up the stairs. Fortunately, one of my friends had a sense of street smarts. She ran down the steps, screaming at the top of her lungs while crying loudly, "Help! Someone please help!"

The last thing I heard the assailant say was, "Your friend shouldn't have done that. She'll pay for that." He quickly walked down the stairs and out of the building, never to be seen again. I knew there was no one home so my other friend and I ran down the stairs, hoping to find someone to help us. We ran outside and noticed our friend was crying to one of my neighbors. I knew the neighbor well. She hugged me and took the three of us to her house. The police were called and a report was filed, but none of it erased the disturbing event of the day from my mind.

I wished Father were on the stairwell of our building to beat up the man who had frightened me so terribly. I was horrified. It took a long time for me to get over the feeling of being victimized. I wanted Father's protection in the past, but this was different. It was the most significant of all the events in my young years, and I had never felt more vulnerable. I began to imagine that every stranger on the street was out to get me, and saw a predator in every man that looked at me. Everything had changed and I never again felt safe in that building.

CHAPTER 9

After a few months, Mother had scolded me several times about my paranoia. I hid much of my fears because I knew no one understood how I felt. When it came to my father, feeling disappointment was pointless so again I kept my thoughts to myself. I did not share my opinion, and barely asked any questions. I had grown tired of secretly wishing Father were there to keep us safe, and had given up on the matter. Life simply went on.

Mother had begun her last year of college. The workload was demanding and, in an effort to spend more time with us, she started a study group. She and three other university students would do much of the school work at our home. Among her friends was a very special man named Oscar. He was from the Dominican Republic and seemed to be interested in Mother. He came over more than anyone else in the study group and slowly developed a relationship with Gabriel and me. He became involved in our lives as Mother's friend.

Mother was too involved in her part-time relationship with Father to openly declare a romance with anyone else. I remember Oscar fondly. He was legitimately interested in our wellbeing. He questioned Mother about Gabriel and me getting the proper nutrition, sometimes took us to the park, and spent as much time as possible in our home. Mother and he obviously had many things in common. They were the same age, which was refreshing for her since Father is 11 years older than Mother and was a widower with a child when they met. Mother was a beautiful woman who had many admirers but she fell in love with Father, an older man, and never gave anyone else a chance.

However, Oscar was special. She never accepted him as anything more than a friend but Gabriel and I knew she enjoyed his company. We thought he might stand a chance if it were not for my grandmother's ruling thumb and my father's grip on her. Oscar, as her dearest friend, would be part of our lives for several years. While Father continued living his double life, Oscar spent all his free time with Mother and us. He was always well mannered and, like Mother, was never involved in behavior that was unbecoming. I loved him and considered him a family member. Nevertheless, Mother and Oscar never had a chance. She was obsessed with Father and blind to any other possibility of finding happiness. It was surprising that he was not discouraged. He loved us and never demanded anything in return.

As years passed, I had grown accustomed to the family's routine weekend parties. Colombians are happy people who will use any excuse as a reason to celebrate. I remember growing up with my extended family as treasured time. We listened to the music of amazing musicians and happily danced and laughed together. We were proud to be Americans but honored and loved our heritage. I was fine with the fact that progress was slow for us in Washington Heights, mainly because I was certain I would miss everyone if Mother finally found the means to move away from the city. I recall the reunions of the grandparents, uncles, aunts, cousins, friends, neighbors… We lived by the motto, "al mal tiempo, buena cara." This meant it did not matter that we had no riches, and it did not matter that everyone struggled to pay rent, food, and all other bills. We were going to celebrate and be happy, regardless. I remember Tia Maria would cook enough rice, beans, steak, and plantains for a hundred people. During one of the celebrations, Mami Abuela's dog, La Pola, forcefully ran into Tia Maria while she was holding a giant bowl, prompting her to drop the steaming hot rice on the floor. She immediately forced Pola out of the kitchen and said to herself, "Ave Maria!" She promptly took action figuring, oh well no problem, and scooped the sticky, dirty rice back into the bowl. She nicely instructed everyone to remove any dog hair from their plate before they ate their meal. These were simple but very good times. The incident served as a family joke for years.

Mother was overly protective and allowed us very little freedom. Apart from enjoying time with our family, she allowed our apartment to evolve from a terrific playground to a teenage gathering place for a select group of neighborhood kids. Pending Mother's approval and her presence at home, our friends would hang out at our apartment. We played board games, watched MTV videos, and listened to the radio. I had replaced the John Travolta and Olivia Newton John posters on the wall for posters of the incredibly gorgeous John Stamos and my favorite punk rock singer, Billy Idol.

We continued to follow the established routine, except now I had developed good cooking skills and always created a shopping list to make certain Gabriel bought the right ingredients at the grocery store. I cooked dinner almost every day. We tried carrying on as we had in the past but ignoring the changes that plagued our neighborhood was becoming increasingly difficult. Mother thought the element was rapidly changing and it was becoming too dangerous for my brother and me to live in Washington Heights. She continued to focus on a plan to buy a home and wanted to move urgently.

Eventually, Father started to stay for longer periods of time with us. I was thirteen years old and about to go into high school when Father informed Mother he would be moving in with us permanently. I watched Mother speak to him like a submissive child. They conversed about the usual nonsense, which I typically ignored.

This time I recall paying attention as she asked, "Octavio, when are you leaving?"

"I'm not. I'm here to stay for good." She did not respond. He never gave Mother or us an opportunity to object. It was a tyrannical imposition. I was baffled and completely frustrated. It was hard to believe she had absolutely no backbone. I sighed loudly and walked away because I expected him to ask for forgiveness or at least ask us if it was acceptable that he move back in permanently. Neither would happen. Shortly after his announcement he traveled to Miami, as he often did. While he was away, I remember Oscar visited our apartment. It was the first time I had ever seen him noticeably inebriated. He cried and begged Mother to reconsider her reconciliation with my father. I felt sad and sorry for him. He had been a good friend to us and he had always secretly loved Mother. He was in an unusual state so Mother requested he leave. He sniffled while he declared his love for her and us. He had invested his time and heart into the relationship and in a swift decision made by Father, he had lost it all. He refused to leave and tried talking Mother into considering him as her life partner instead. I watched as he dozed off on the old sofa, part of me wishing Mother had opened her heart to him. He was respectful and considerate, and I believed him worthy of our affection. I wonder if Oscar and Mother would have married... How would our lives be different? The only thing I understood was that she had robbed herself of the opportunity of a new relationship with a man that offered unconditional love and respect.

Mother asked that I keep Oscar's visit and the entire incident a secret. "Josefina, do not say a word about this to your father. He would be furious if he knew about our relationship with Oscar." Although I didn't understand why her relationship with a person who had been so important in our lives was a secret, I made the promise and kept my word. I believed Father did not have the right to dictate whether or not Oscar should be our friend, nor should he be upset since he had failed us in so many ways, so many times. I didn't understand the double standard but I was left with no choice but to respect her wishes.

My parents' reconciliation meant Mother's dream of moving out of Washington Heights would soon come true. We looked for a new house in a better neighborhood where Father's previous absence could be completely erased. He would be a permanent resident, stealing some of the magic from our lives. Mixed emotions plagued my young mind. On the one hand, it was time for change. I still felt fear about my unfortunate experience and wanted to leave the building, and I did love Father when he was around. On the other hand, he had failed us repeatedly and it was difficult to trust him. It seemed like the change came with the high price of having to constantly deal with the man who had deserted us. In the end, none of what was in store for our future was up to Gabriel, or me; not even Mother, for that matter. She had replaced her democratic system for a totalitarian regime.

After a couple of months, we went on a joy ride on the Staten Island Ferry. Father drove his dark blue Buick onto the ferry platform and parked it. The thirty-minute boat ride to Staten Island was a wonderful eye-opener for me. Although we had lived in the city for several years, I was enjoying the awe-inspiring beauty of the New York Harbor on a boat for the first time. The air was crisp, the sky was clear; essentially nothing interfered with the spectacular image of south Manhattan's magnificent skyscrapers, historic bridges, the iconic Statue of Liberty, and the infamous Ellis Island, which all made for a remarkable day trip.

We drove off the ferry and drove around Staten Island. It occurred to my parents that this might be the perfect place to relocate. It was close to New York City, allowing Mother to keep her job as an accountant at a firm that operated out of Broadway, across Union Square Park in south Manhattan. The small company specialized in providing energy to heat homes. Mother's boss was a very nice man who was raised by a single mom and was considerate of Mother's status, allowing her special privileges. For instance, we could visit the office and have lunch with the staff during the summers. He was a patient man, tolerant of Mother's broken English, and appreciated her gift as an exceptional accountant.

I have many fond memories related to Mother's job, particularly the established yearly routine of meeting our mother at least one day after work during Christmastime. We would choose a day and plan a subway trip after school to Mother's job to do the Christmas shopping in my beloved New York City. The experience was beyond compare for me. The city was a winter wonderland and I believe there's truly no place like it on earth. I could breathe the festivity, the smell of roasted nuts mixed with the bitter cold breeze, and the large crowds all with the same mission of finding the perfect gift for their loved ones. I loved looking at the Christmas window displays and the red nosed Santa Claus on every other corner, ringing the bells atop the Salvation Army donation buckets. New Yorkers spreading cheer, the lights, the hot chocolate – all of it was exhilarating, even the unpleasant stench and heat that rose from the subway.

We canvassed areas throughout Staten Island in hopes of finding our next home. My parents thought this bedroom community was appealing because it was the least populated of New York City's five boroughs, and it seemed like the perfect place to enjoy living in a safer suburban environment while Mother could remain relatively close to her place of employment. I, too, wanted to give Staten Island a chance. Mother proposed, "Josefina, Gabriel, we could stay close to the city we love and be in a place that will give us a new life, far from the dangers of the inner city." It made sense to us. I knew our approval was unnecessary, but I appreciated her efforts. Gabriel and I wanted to be team players so we both agreed to begin the search for a new home.

CHAPTER 10

Staten Island

We would visit Staten Island a few times before my parents closed the deal on a two-family house in a "middle class" neighborhood. Mother wanted tenants to offset some of the financial obligations that came with buying a new home since she felt uncertain of Father's overall stability and was always cautious when it related to her finances. The house they decided to purchase already had a family renting the second floor. My parents decided to keep the tenants since the previous owner stated they were a nice family who always paid the rent on time.

"Truck is loaded! Let's go! Move it! It's getting late!" Mother yelled. Gabriel and I grabbed the last few books off the floor, and I could hear him obediently sprint down the steps. Before walking out the door, I felt compelled to turn back and give a last homage to the place I loved. An irresistible nostalgia crept in as I stood by my bedroom door and glanced at the black linings on the walls, markings left behind by the posters that provided years of decorative service. I walked by the second bedroom door and glanced at the old fire escape mounted on the side of our building, the steel play area where we spent countless hours talking, singing, and playing, now seemed rusty and old. I thought about our next door neighbor, Sol, and how we took turns bringing snacks to our favorite hang-out while we dreamed the way little girls dream. I turned my head and noticed the quiet, small paint-chipped radiator. I chuckled because it was never strong enough to warm up our apartment. Instead, it served a much more important purpose. For years it kept Mother's food warm while she worked long hours. It also dried our snow soaked socks after we removed them from our near frostbitten feet. A flood of memories flashed in my head. The friends we were leaving behind, the church that had sheltered me from many disillusions, the family gatherings, the Spanish restaurants... I even thought I'd miss the local laundromat that I had hated.

I felt crushed and was aware that Mother had raised the white flag. An enemy force invaded our lives, obstructing her personal growth with disregard to past sacrifice. She was the lone soldier in the Big Apple battlefield, and a more astute warrior armed with a house in a suburban landfill had shamelessly slaughtered the naïve private. I took a mental picture of the old place and hoped that the new beginnings would be good enough to replace it.

The drive was about an hour long. Mother and I followed Father in the family car, while he, accompanied by Gabriel, drove the U-Haul truck. I was reluctant to embrace any excitement, but Mother seemed animated by the start of this new phase in our lives. We shared thoughts on how we would fix our new place and had mostly small talk before we left Manhattan. I didn't want Mother to think I was being dramatic about this new change, so I remained fairly quiet for most of the trip. By the time we arrived at the new house I had experienced the five stages of acceptance. Staten Island was our new home and it was now time to move forward.

Father parked the truck in front of the ordinary-looking house on James Court while Mother looked for a parking spot that wouldn't be in the way of the truck. I immediately noticed a tire park across the street from the house. The swings were made out of black rubber tires, the slide landing was a black rubber tire, the seesaw had black rubber tires placed in the middle, and the play area was fenced by rubber tires. I've never seen a more distasteful park. I asked myself, "What kid would want to play there?" I saw a neighbor walking his dog in the black rubber tire park and sarcastically mentioned how the park was probably flea infested. Mother gave me an exasperated look that reminded me I was being negative. I got out of the car and walked toward our new house.

The driveway had an oddly steep incline. If Mother had parked the car there, it would have easily exposed the car's undercarriage. To the right of the driveway there was a short walkway to the front entrance, and to the right of the walkway a small grassy area that bordered our neighbor's house. There were three steps that led to a small front porch on the left, and two single wooden doors on the right. The front exterior wall of the first floor had a brick surface layer that wrapped around the oversized bay window located in the center of the front porch. The rest of the house's exterior was made up of white vertical panels, a wood-like plastic composite in need of a power wash. The front door on the left side led to the entrance of the first floor of the house. This was where we would live.

I went through the front door into the open-space design with the living room and dining room area to the left, and to the right there was a small entrance to the kitchen. The kitchen had light wood cabinets and a window big enough to let in the bright daylight. I walked further, past the dining room to a short hallway where there was a standard size bedroom on the left with a bathroom directly across from it. I continued to walk down the hallway and saw the pink colored walls of the second bedroom. It would be easy to claim this bigger room as mine. I knew Gabriel would want nothing to do with a pink room. Next to my room was the master bedroom. It was a nice size and it included its own private full bathroom. This was a nice change for Mother. She could finally have her own private bathroom.

After taking a quick scan of the rooms, I walked back to the hallway and into the kitchen. There was a side door that opened to a staircase, which led down to access the finished basement. The basement had gray-colored, industrial looking walls. It felt damp and cold and appeared to have little or no functionality. It housed the laundry machines, which were placed on a high platform. We would soon find out the platform was necessary to protect the machines from the frequent flooding after a significant rainstorm. It turned out that water naturally drained down the abnormally steep driveway and flowed effortlessly through the garage door and into the basement.

I walked back upstairs and out the front door. Mother was speaking to our tenant, a lady who seemed very nice and invited us to take a peek at the upstairs apartment. She opened the door on the right and we all followed her up the stairs leading to the second floor. The layout was exactly the same as ours. She kept it nicely decorated and very clean. My disappointment diminished a bit, because I could see our place had the potential to look beautiful. I tried to change my perspective on the house but it was difficult to ignore the vertical driveway, the moldy garage, and the damp, cold basement. The architecture seemed impractical but I could tell the living space had some appeal after all. I thought my parents had valid reasons to move there, so the least I could do is be appreciative and value their investment.

Our tenant welcomed us to the neighborhood and introduced us to her daughters. I was glad the place was rented to a nice family. The two daughters were around my same age, and I was glad my parents had agreed to allow the family to continue renting after we purchased the house. They seemed like nice people and I thought the girls were potential friends.

After a short visit we all said thank you to our tenant and walked back down the stairs to the outside. I continued the inspection of what was beginning to look like a nice place, and then I walked to the back yard. I couldn't believe how messy it all seemed. There were dried up brown bushes and a tall grassy area in obvious need of trimming, mixed with dirt. The soil was apparently unfertile since there were no plants flourishing, just a few ugly weeds. There was a half empty, deflated blue plastic pool filled with dirt and dead leaves. I wondered why someone would leave this damaged piece of plastic laying there to rot.

"Josefina!"

"Yes Mother?"

"We need help. Where are you?"

"I'm coming..."

I ran back to the front and briefly noticed a girl walking out of the house next door. In passing we made eye contact. I noticed her heavy mascara accentuated her clear blue eyes. Neither one of us was forthcoming in saying hello. She walked by with little acknowledgement of my presence. I thought about how difficult the move had been and hoped she would not turn out to be stuck up and unfriendly. I went on to help unload the truck and empty out boxes in the house. Moving was time consuming and exhausting. I was relieved we didn't have much furniture from the old apartment since my parents were replacing the old stuff. Still, it would take a few days to get completely organized.

Along with our move to Staten Island came the start of my first year of high school. A couple days after our move, I spent a day visiting the local public high school. The metal detectors and smoking rooms for teachers and students made the place seem more like a low security prison than a school. I was appalled. I sat in a so-called study hall where kids did everything but study. I felt out of place, an odd ball! I did not want to be a student in this school. It was scary to think this may be where I might have to spend the next four academic years of my life. The disorganization and lack of academic appeal made me think to myself, "Wow! Metal detectors, smoking rooms, so much freedom. I hate it!" I guess I was truly a dork.

Although there were security guards on premise, I didn't feel safe and the "teachers" walking in and out of classrooms gave the impression they wanted to be there less than the kids did. I left the school building that afternoon feeling discouraged. I had been the kid who loved school, who would not miss a day even when I wasn't feeling well. Now I couldn't imagine having to go back to that unstructured, cold place. I sat in a classroom during the last class of the day, plotting on ways to quit school. Finally, the dismissal bell rang. I rushed out of the building along with the other unenthusiastic learners and saw Father's car parked in front of the school. I had never been happier to see him. It had dawned on me that I wasn't certain which bus I'd have to take home, and after such a depressing day I was grateful I didn't have to. I opened the door of the car.

Sporting a happy smile he said, "Hello Josefina, how was your day?"

I instinctively responded, "Terrible! I hate this place! It's like a prison in there with metal detectors, security officers. Teachers don't seem to care about their students! I wish I were back in the city."

He started laughing, "Aww, my poor girl."

"Why are you laughing?"

"Josefina, after I dropped you off this morning, I knew you'd hate this place. I searched for the Catholic schools in the area, found a place I know you'll love, and registered you. It is a regional Catholic school located near the Staten Island ferry."

I abruptly let out a thrilled scream. Father put his hand on his chest and exclaimed, "Josefina, what's wrong with you? I almost crashed!"

"Oh, my gosh! You are the greatest dad a girl could ever want! Love you Daddy! Thank you so much! I'm so, so, so, happy!"

Father laughed, "Good! I knew you'd be happy, so let's go to the uniform store." Dad and I purchased a couple of navy blue polyester pants and a few white blouses. I was excited about high school and couldn't wait to catch up. The academic year had begun a couple of days earlier and I was afraid of falling behind. As we arrived back at the house, I was about to go in the house when I noticed my next-door neighbor turned the corner onto James Court. She was wearing the very same uniform I had just purchased. I felt a brief discontent because I had the impression she was snobbish from our first brief encounter. She was my neighbor so I hoped she wasn't in my grade level. I figured if we avoided one another then we would avoid any future problems. I was excited about starting high school so I quickly dismissed all thoughts about her.

I had difficulty falling asleep that night. The next morning I jumped out of bed before the alarm could go off, took a quick shower and brushed my teeth. I noticed my hair was the longest I had ever had it. I put it up in a ponytail and walked out of the bathroom. I smelled the eggs and toast Father had made Gabriel and me for breakfast. He was an early riser and was fully dressed, ready to drop us off at school. He had registered Gabriel in a Catholic elementary school near my high school. Gabriel was entering the eighth grade and hated having been pulled out on his last elementary school year. Although he did not mind the public school system, Catholic education was important to Mother. He was fine with attending whatever school our parents chose.

Father said, "Josefina, I'll take you to school today, but you need to learn the bus schedule so you can take it tomorrow."

"Ok, thanks."

"I made you breakfast."

I wasn't hungry, but I didn't want to be rude. He had gone through the trouble of making it so I felt obligated to eat. I responded very unenthusiastically, "Ok, thanks." I sat and ate as slowly as I could.

Father became impatient and nicely said, "If you're not hungry, just go get your backpack, we're leaving. I don't want you to be late today."

"I'm ready, and my backpack is by the front door."

"Ok then! Gabriel, go get your stuff. Let's go!"

I was quietly thinking about how the day might turn out as Father drove me to school. I didn't speak much, so Father asked, "Are you alright?"

"Yes, I'm so happy you registered me at a Catholic school. I really didn't like the public school yesterday. Thanks Dad."

"Oh, I'm so happy – I know this is the right place for you. I remember how much you loved your school in New York." About fifteen minutes later Father said, "Here we are, have a good day Josefina. Love you sweetheart."

"Love you Dad."

Father dropped me off at the front of a small building. I immediately felt at home. It was perfect! I loved my dad so much in that moment. I thought maybe I had been hard and unforgiving toward him in the past, so I promised myself to make it a point to always remember that on that day he was exactly the kind of dad I needed him to be. He was mindful enough to make it possible for me to remain in what I considered my safe haven. I felt protected and loved by him. For that brief moment, I accepted that his problems with Mother had nothing to do with me. I thought about how I would be a good daughter to him no matter what their differences.

As soon as I opened the car door I could hear the morning bell ring. I ran up the center staircase, opened one of the large front doors of the three-story building, and ran inside. Stepping inside the building was similar to traveling back in time. I could tell the facility was over a hundred years old and designed with materials meant to endure the test of time. It had crown molding and wood paneling representative of a distinguished era when labor was done by proud people who wanted to impress their creative talents on their finished work. I could tell the durable materials were meant to withstand the adversity of the coldest winters and hottest summers. I recognized a sort of traditional old library book smell mixed with a hint of burning heat rising from the old furnaces. The entrance had an unmistakable character that inspired learning. It didn't have much lighting or ventilation but I felt at home.

The day before, the school principal had informed Father that the student body was composed of a little over four hundred girls and the teachers were mostly nuns. The office had given Father all the paperwork I needed to bring back on my first day of class. I was prepared with my schedule but had to stop by the school office to hand in the paperwork and get directions to my classroom. The school secretary guided me to the second floor and then to the first classroom on the left. I ran up, opened the classroom door, and there she was, sitting on the first row, closest to the door. I silently thought, "Oh great! What are the odds?"

She looked at me but didn't seem to recognize me. I walked in, gave my teacher a note from the office. She introduced me as a new student and asked that I quietly find a seat. I walked to the back of the room where I had noticed an empty spot. I was distracted with my neighbor's presence and hoped she wasn't in all my classes. The bell rang at the end of the period, and my next-door neighbor walked toward the back of the classroom and approached me. "Hey, aren't you the girl who lives next door to me?"

I responded, "Yes, I recognize you also. My name is Josefina."

"Hi, my name is Dana. Welcome to the neighborhood and the school."

"Thanks Dana! So glad to meet you." I was relieved that she had taken the initiative. I thought she'd be a troublemaker and was glad that I was wrong.

Dana gave me some insight on how things worked at the school. For instance, she taught me all the nicknames students had given the nuns at the school. She laughed as she said, "Remember, Josefina, you must walk out of the classroom on the right and follow the guided lines through the hallways unless you want Sister "Patrol" to grab you by the ear and send you to the office." Dana thought some of the rules were ridiculous. I was a borderline nerd who silently disagreed, but laughed because I didn't want to be an outcast over silly jokes.

The classrooms had large windows that extended almost to the ceiling. Buses and cars passed frequently through the busy avenue in front of the building. North of the road was a small, grassy area with benches that faced the river. The view of New York City was spectacular, distracting, and wonderful. I fought daydreaming about taking trips on the ferry or being the boat captain that navigated the ships through the narrow upper bay waters of New York City. I watched the small tugboats that hauled large cargo ships near New Jersey, and the birds that circled the area as they fished day after day. The sun reflected on what I knew was filthy water. The light's impact transformed its murky appearance, creating a mirror-like river of smooth crystal ripples, a dreamlike of waves that crashed into the wall by the road in front of the classroom window. I never tired of the vision. Wise teachers drew the window shades down and stole the show. I valued the discipline since I did not want to struggle and was genuinely interested in making academic gains.

Dana seemed to know everyone. She was very nice and introduced me to all her friends at school and by our neighborhood. She invited me to come along to some of our classmate's parties and school functions.

Living in Staten Island felt normal and right; it was easy to embrace this new life. We all grew accustomed to the new schedules. Mother routinely took the local bus to the Staten Island Ferry and, upon arriving in Manhattan, she would take a train to 14th Street for work. I helped around the house and was too busy with my schoolwork to pay any mind to what was going on outside of my immediate scope. My brother and I went to school while Father continued with his erratic schedule. He spent most days at home and sometimes would go out at night. In Manhattan his dealings were easily ignored. People in the city were too busy, too self-involved to notice each other's occupational practices. The Staten Islanders had a small town mentality, very different than what I was used to. Most of the men in the neighborhood were blue-collar workers except for Dana's father, who worked on Wall Street. I knew our tenant worked for the sanitation department, and our next-door neighbor drove a truck.

There were others on our block that were construction workers, firemen, and police officers. Around the corner there were a few low-grade proud "wanna be" gangsters. We were the new family in town and evidently the neighbors were curious and somewhat suspicious of Father's occupation. He was obviously not a typical working man and, although I tried not to ponder the matter, avoiding answering the most frequently asked question out of every neighbor's mouth, "What does your dad do for a living?" was a struggle. It seemed impossible for these nosey people to ignore each other's business. Father finally instructed us to tell people he owned a camera shop. His associate in Queens owned a camera shop, which he used as a front for his dealings. I was desensitized to the reality of Father's business so I appreciated the phony solution. I supposed being your own boss provided a legitimate explanation once and for all as to why he had such an unusual schedule. The sham relieved the pressure of having to make up fancy lies that could snowball to additional questions and additional lies.

My darling cat, Baby, seemed to be instantly content with the geographical change and had easily adapted to her new environment. At the end of my first spring in Staten Island, I sat on the front porch to read while she sat and purred next to me. Baby stared at everything and nothing. I was engrossed in my book when I heard the sound of sneakers hitting the pavement. I looked up and noticed it was a young man jogging across the street from the house. He stopped directly in front of the tire park and surprised me when he walked across the road and over to where I was.

"Hello!"

"Hi."

"I'm Sam. I live around the corner from here. Did you just move in?"

"Yeah, a couple of months ago."
"What's your name?"

"Josefina."

"I grew up here so I knew you were new to the neighborhood. How do you like it so far?"

"It's fine. It's nice and quiet."

"Quiet? Where are you from?"

"I moved here from Manhattan."

"No, I mean you have a bit of an accent."

"Oh, I'm Colombian."

"Nice! You're the first Colombian I've ever met."

There were plenty of Colombians in the city so I didn't know what to say. I thought to myself, "Did this guy just crawl from under a rock?" I didn't want to be rude so I gave him a fake smile.

At first sight he seemed like a bit of a troublemaker. He was dressed like a rocker, wearing a Led Zeppelin t-shirt and blue jeans. This was different for me. I had grown up around boys that were into the Run DMC hip-hop look.

Kids in the city cared about music, dancing, and their sneakers. Even Gabriel, who was typically easy to please, made a big deal about buying the latest sneaker models on the market. A couple of years earlier he had demanded a new Adidas model, which was sold out in most shoe stores across Manhattan. Mother granted him this one fad and willingly drove all around New York City looking for the exact pair he wanted, no matter the cost. It took almost two whole days before we finally found the shoes. I was so aggravated by his persistence but I also knew he was otherwise an easygoing kid. I sat in the front passenger seat of the car while Mother drove around and Gabriel jumped in and out of the car to make his inquiries. I felt delighted when we found the pair he wanted. I must admit it was great to see how happy he was to finally get his wish.

Sam was not wearing exercise apparel so I got the impression he used jogging as an excuse to come over and say hello. Growing up in the city demanded certain precautions. At first I was apprehensive toward anyone I did not know. I don't know what about Sam's appearance gave me the impression he was a bit of a troublemaker, but as he continued to talk, I felt less bothered.

"Josefina, that's a nice name. How old are you? What do you do for fun?"

I thought. "Wow! Aren't you curious?" but kept it to myself.

"I just turned fifteen. You?"

"I'm seventeen. So, you're a freshman in high school?"

"Yes. You?"

"No, I don't go to school. I want to make money so I work full-time. They don't teach you much in school anyway. It's pointless."

I glanced at my book, indicating I wanted to go back to my reading.

He must have noticed how disagreeable being a high school dropout was to me. After a short pause, I answered, "I read for fun."

"Anyway, I live around the corner from your house. I'm sure I'll be seeing you around."

"Yeah, I'll see you around."

Sam was a little over six feet tall. He had a medium build, kept in good shape, and I noticed his butt when he turned to walk away. I remember thinking he had a nice butt. His striking blue eyes and plump red lips were captivating, but I did not find his blonde hair particularly attractive. Despite the short conversation, I could tell he was personable. He had an enigmatic and appealing coolness about him, a kind of bad boy flare. I liked personality more than any physical attribute in a person, so after he walked away, I thought about our short conversation. I found his interest in speaking to me flattering, perhaps because I was young and slightly impressionable.

Sam often walked by my house and made the effort to stop by and talk. He seemed to really enjoy sitting on the porch next to Baby and me. I didn't have any experience with boys and wasn't thinking of him as anything more than a friend. At first, I just thought he knew the neighborhood and the people and that our friendship would ease my transition into the new place. I welcomed his company without any preconceived ideas of developing a romantic relationship.

The last time I had an interest in a boy was in the 7th grade. His name was Angel. My best friend and I had a crush on him but, for the sake of our friendship, we agreed that neither one of us would bother with him. It was really disappointing when my best friend betrayed this agreement and admitted they had gone to the movies together. I decided to end the friendship, partly because I had picked up on some of Mother's beliefs about women's competitive nature as being conniving, and partly because I felt betrayed. From that point forward I thought boys differed from girls in a good way. They had a healthier competitive nature and were much less complicated as friends. I suppose carrying my mother's mistrust of other women influenced my overreaction to the insignificant rivalry between two schoolgirls. Right or wrong, I was cautious around other girls and felt most comfortable in the company of guy friends. In hindsight, I realize legitimate female friendships serve as a source of support and empowerment. I mistakenly blamed that trivial incident for the lack of trust I had toward women in general. I've since come to realize that women can help one another find a sense of communal belonging, but as a young girl I had trust issues as it related to my gender. I also had no patience for the emotional drama my girlfriends thrived in. Up until this point I had made the choice to stay away from as much "girl" gossip and fuss as possible. Most of my friends growing up were boys, mainly because I had a tremendous love for sports and felt a commonality with their no-nonsense, let's go get 'em attitude.

Now I was a teenager and I instinctively felt things were slowly changing. At first, I thought of Sam as one more of my friends, and was aloof to his interest in me. My apathy was not a deterrent for him; he continued to stop by my house and spend a significant amount of time trying to win my affection. He spoke to me freely, and shared his thoughts on his family and his life goals. He worked at a video store owned by his neighbor, a man named John whom he considered a good friend. He enjoyed working at the video store because it gave him the opportunity to meet many people. Sam thought of every person as a potential connection. He was smart but had no interest in school. He believed his entrepreneurial mindset was his ticket to success. He was serious about wanting to make money and thought working at the video store helped him create a trusting relationship with his boss.

John, a successful man in his late twenties, could potentially provide Sam with valuable insight on how to create wealth. Sam's eagerness to learn as much as he could from John was appealing. For a while, Sam and I were in complete synch. He was inquisitive, intelligent, and ambitious. In the past, I appreciated every experience I had with the finer things, and believed that if I was wealthy I could enjoy all those things at will. I loved the scent of expensive perfumes at the fragrance department in Saks Fifth Avenue and admired the beautiful models wearing fur coats on the cover of Vogue magazine.

I also enjoyed watching the TV series "Dynasty". The glamour of the Carrington family was intriguing to me. I thought Sam could be a self-made man similar to the main character, Blake Carrington. Blake's eccentric personality possessed a fearless quality. He was impressionable, as attaining financial success was an everyday accomplishment for him. I followed the character's evolution carefully. Initially, he had a bit of good luck but it was his razor sharp determination that motivated his competitiveness and ultimately helped him reached his success. I was inexperienced and had never met someone close to my age that was ambitious. I contemplated many fantasies and ideas about how Sam could be a future Blake Carrington. With every passing day, I began to expect and look forward to Sam's advances to the point of developing an attraction and desire for his company. He would share with me stories of his personal struggles, mainly regarding his parents' divorce. He lived with his sister and his single mom, and felt responsible for them. They were the motivation that encouraged and fed his aspiring nature. I presume the common experience of dysfunctional homes, our desires, and our mutual craving for material things were the basis of our connection and the seed to our future romance.

Mother was what we called "old school", which really meant she was very strict. She did not allow me to go out on dates alone with Sam.

He respected Mother's rules and was happy to hang out at the house with Gabriel and me. I had felt confident I would fit in since I had always been a popular girl, and there was no reason to believe things would be any different; however, I admit that Sam played an instrumental part in my quickly adapting to Staten Island. I began to enjoy the quietness and the people of this "small" town. I felt like a normal teenager, and with every passing day the neighborhood, the house, the people, Sam, all of it began to steadily grow on me. I quickly became popular with all my new friends, in school and in the neighborhood.

With our move came a more relaxed environment. My parents became a little less vigilant of my every move. Gabriel and I were involved with school projects, sports, new friends, and so on... Mother was busy commuting, working, organizing, and adjusting to our new life, and so on... Father was also busy doing much work around the house, whatever else, and so on...

On a day like any other, Sam invited Dana and me to his dad's house in Brooklyn. He was on his way and thought it would be nice that we meet his father. Dana's parents were not strict, so she was allowed more freedom than I. She did not hesitate, "Oh cool! I'll go for a ride."

I did not want to seem childlike so, without hesitation, I accepted the invitation. "Yeah, that's fine." I did not feel worried. I knew I could go places during the day without Mother's awareness, and Father was busy doing his own thing and would probably not ask any questions. I felt important relating to someone who was slightly older, someone who drove his own car. I was excited, not nervous, as I sat in the front passenger seat, with Dana sitting in the back. Sam drove on the Staten Island Expressway and across the Verrazano-Narrows Bridge into the Belt Parkway. It was the first time I had left the neighborhood without my family. It was an intimidating and, at the same time exhilarating, journey. I looked at the bridge's suspension cords and thought of the marvel of it all. I could see Manhattan and Brooklyn, and the many cars that were speeding alongside ours. I was in the front seat and I felt liberated and adventurous. We arrived at Sam's father's to discover he was not home. Sam thought his father probably forgot he was visiting and might have gone out with his girlfriend. Sam waited a few minutes before he became impatient and decided to return to Staten Island. The disappointment did not matter to me. The trip marked a milestone in my life. It was my first recollection of an event that opened a window into grown up life so that I could take a short peek. It changed how I felt about everything.

Dana and I were now best friends, and my relationship with Sam intensified. I felt he was someone I could trust and be mischievous with. After we got back home I said goodnight to Dana and Sam. A few minutes after I went in the house, Sam called me. "Hello?"

"Josefina, I want to know if you like me as much as I like you."

My heart skipped a beat. "Yes, I think you know I do."

Sam went on and said, "Ok then, let's officially become a couple. I want you to be my girlfriend."

"Sam, I want that too."

"Josefina, go outside. I'll walk over to your house. I'll be there in a minute."

"Right now? Ok." I noticed Father was cooking and Mother was reading in her room. I quietly opened the front door and saw Sam almost at the front of my house.

He signaled that we walk to the side of the house. I barely walked down the three steps by the front door when he grabbed my hand and, like a little rascal, led me to where there were no windows. He had a look on his face as if he was about to teach me something good. I was the eager learner with butterflies in my stomach. He put both hands on my face and pressed his lips against mine.

Instinctively, we both opened our mouths. It was a kiss with tongue! My face was flushed. Sam stepped back a little and looked at me. In a whisper he asked, "Are you embarrassed?" He didn't wait for a response. "I know your parents are home, so I'll let you go back in the house." He gave me another soft kiss, and said, "I'm so happy we're exclusive."

These were strange words. Exclusive? The thought of seeing other people had never crossed my mind but I embraced the idea that he had declared our relationship official. I was excited and could barely sleep that night. I played the scene over and over in my mind, and giggled at the image of him taking my hand and swiftly controlling the walk to the side of the house.

In a short amount of time Sam and I became inseparable. He was an influential person in my life. I considered him an open minded, striving man, and I enjoyed his charming ways. He never wasted an opportunity to compliment me. I was glad I had finally grown my hair because he would run his fingers through my long, black hair and whisper in my ear, "All of you is unique and beautiful." I melted at his tone and soft gesture. He compared me to a Hawaiian princess because of my brown, slightly slanted eyes. He liked my height, which was cool since I had an issue with always having been the tallest girl in my class. I am unusually tall for a Spanish woman. My long limbs and fine, lengthy fingers would not go unnoticed by Sam. He claimed they were an indication of royal elegance. My breasts were large and I had a curvy figure for a thin teenager. He was not shy to compliment my small waist and claimed it heightened my round butt. Sam often stated that he loved every part of me. We clicked in so many ways. We talked about our greatest disappointments, fears, achievements, and shortcomings. We played board games with Dana and Gabriel, and talked outside my house for hours. I felt we were mentally connected. He was respectful of me and had moved slowly. There were times where part of me was confused about whether it was Sam or my raging hormones at work, but I began to think about advancing the physical aspect of our relationship. He ignited a sensual curiosity in me that I couldn't wait to explore.

Initially, his friendship was a better option to being bored and lonely in a new place, but we had come a long way. Sam had transformed our friendship into what I believed was love. Not only did I enjoy kissing him but something about him had become essential to me. I felt ready to explore sex, and I knew engaging intimately with him was only a matter of time.

CHAPTER 11

My freshman year was over very quickly. I couldn't believe how fast it had gone by but I was definitely ready for the summer of 1985. Our apartment in New York City had no air conditioner. For Gabriel, Mother and me, summers meant we'd suffer three months of inescapable heat. I had looked forward to experiencing our new central air-conditioning unit but Gabriel played with the thermostat constantly. Sometimes he lowered the temperature so much that it made the place bitter cold. I would scream at him, "Please! Raise the temperature in this igloo! My bones hurt and I need a little warmth!" He would say, "Hell, no! I love it and you're not changing it!" I would push him to try to get to the thermostat but he would always overpower me. I reminded him I was his older sister and that he needed to listen, but he never took me seriously. I tried pushing him around as if he was still shorter and weaker, but he had taken up sports and was seriously stronger than me. He would push me down until I was facing the ground and would pull my underpants up so high from the back that I'd always end up begging for mercy. I didn't find his stupid games funny. I thought I was too old for such childish behavior but he'd always laugh for so long that I'd end up forgiving him and laughing along with him. He was a wise guy, "Josefina, I bet you feel warm now! Hahahaha! Not yet? You must want more!" He'd slap me on the forehead, call out the word "Biff!" and run. Neither one of us knew what the word "Biff" meant but we'd use it every time we slapped each other's forehead. I realized he was faster and stronger so I would spend most of the day looking for an opportunity to revenge his painful games. I'd carry on a grudge for hours and when he least expected it, I would get a perfect lucky shot, square in the middle of his forehead "Biff!" and would enjoy a short victory dance while I ran as fast as I could. He'd always catch me but I didn't care; getting body slammed had become part of the fun, although I was realizing he was getting too strong for me to continue playing any games that involved physical force.

We'd never take it too seriously but someone almost always ended up getting hurt. Once I meant to slap his forehead and instead got him square in the face. He started crying because Mother had always stated a man's face was sacred and that no one should ever slap it. I felt terrible and ended up crying along with him and apologizing repeatedly. He took a long while to calm down so I took a glass of cold water and threw it at his face while repeating the words, "Breathe, just breathe!"

Well, he never got my good intention so he looked at me with determined eyes and said, "Oh! You've gone too far now! You're going to get it!" I saw the seriousness in his face and ran for cover. We both knew the days of playing with water balloons in the house were over but it did not stop him from chasing me around the living room couch and down the steps to the basement. I saw Baby's metal brush on the washing machine and, without giving it too much thought, I quickly grabbed the brush and with unpredictable force, jammed it into his back as he was ready to body slam me. I'll never forgive myself! I saw blood drip down the back of his t-shirt! "OH, NO! Gabriel! I'm sorry! I didn't mean it! I swear!" We looked at one another and knew that that was enough. We both cried inconsolably and promised we wouldn't tell Mother. Later that day, he grew tired of watching me cry and accepted my apology. We loved each other and never held any resentment. I felt so guilty about hurting him that I decided it would be the last time my brother and I would play that way.

I felt energized by the summer sunshine. It had replaced the brownish weeds into the most radiant greenery in our backyard. The plastic pool had long been thrown away, giving the grass an opportunity to grow out. Staten Island was a newfound paradise for me. I looked around the house and appreciated all the work Mother had done to make this place a comfy home. She painted the house in soft pastel colors, treating each room with special care. In the dining room area she used track lighting. She wanted the fixtures to complement the mirrored wall, which gave the house a contemporary look. She purchased a trendy but enormous glass top lacquer-framed table, which took up considerable space but looked lovely. The table's glossy, black finish with matching chairs was part of a set that included an elegant china cabinet with sleek, black lacquer sideboards decorated with gold hardware and trim. Although the furniture pieces took up most of the dining room space, at the time it was a chic look. Our fashionable living room furniture had deep maroon-colored couches and chairs. They were large, puffy, bulky, a true representation of the 80's. The sturdy black-framed coffee table had a glass top, which complemented all the other pieces, and the soft gray rug was the final touch.

Mother hung a couple of Fernando Botero lithographs Father had brought to the states from Colombia. Mother loved the artist's signature style "Boterismo" where he portrays heavyset people and figures. She bragged about his being a native of Medellin. She thought it was a refreshing change to have someone represent Colombia in a good light. The bay window had pastel-colored vertical blinds, which were kept open most of the time. Our kitchen had light colored wood cabinets and laminate flooring. The country style, eat-in kitchen table didn't seem to tie in with any of the other rooms in the house but Mother thought it went well with the cabinets.

My parents had a classy, black lacquered deco-style bed frame. It had curves at the ends with gold trim. The glamorous headboard had a lit mirror that extended from one end to the other. On its frame there was a built-in radio in the center with two speakers, one near each end of the piece. Above the radio Mother kept the dim night-lights on. The nightstands had gold pulls and some gold floral accents, giving the room a dramatic look.

My bedroom was a typical girl room with strawberry sherbet-like pink walls. My bed did not have a headboard; it was flush against the wall. I used accent pillows and way too many stuffed animals to decorate it. My nightstand was a plain white lacquer piece with two draws. The rug in my room was lime green which was loud, unattractive, and didn't match anything, but my parents thought it was in good shape and refused to replace it. I continued to use pictures and posters to decorate my walls. I loved the mirrored closet doors because I could see myself from head to toe before walking out the door. This was important because I had started to care more about my appearance. I'd routinely stare at the long mirrors and change my outfits multiple times before leaving the house. Nevertheless, my most prized possession was a small record player I had placed on a small desk near my door. I often played Cyndi Lauper's song "Girls Just Want to Have Fun". I practically lived every word of that song! I loved her outfits and often tried to imitate her look, especially her wild hair. I jumped up and down as I sang along; it was a fun way to get excited for the day ahead.

I had fully transitioned into my new life. I was feeling unusually happy on a particular evening when I stepped outside the house. An unfamiliar soothing breeze created an aromatherapy produced by the blossoming white jasmine that seemed to have sprouted instantaneously from our shrubs. I lost myself while smelling their inexplicably hypnotizing aroma and observing their simple yet universal beauty, a fragile flower that emanated an enormously soothing fragrance, bringing a euphoric calmness unlike anything I had ever felt before.

For the first time, I believed this new place had the potential to replace my beloved New York City. My parents' saga no longer mattered much to me. They seemed to get along for the most part. Father was home on most days and he made a really great Mom and cooked wonderful meals. I was ecstatic that the Chef Boyardee days were over. He drove us around and made sure that we had everything we needed. He even attended Gabriel's football games. Sometimes he picked me up after school and gave my friends a ride home. He didn't mind taking Dana and I to the mall or to the movie theatre, or to watch basketball games at school. He spoke to me about school functions and we really started to bond.

I still remember how happy I felt at the end of my freshman year when my dad and I went to the Father-Daughter school dance. My dad was very charming and knew how to make me feel really special. He wore a tuxedo, bought me a beautiful dress, and even remembered to get me a pink corsage. He was a complete gentleman, opened the car door for me, and told me I was his little princess. His chivalry was probably what made him popular with women. He taught me to expect a man to be courteous while in my presence. Father didn't just confuse Mother, he confused me as well. I wanted someone who was gentle and attentive like Father, but someone who would only have eyes for me, unlike Father. He always represented so many contradictions, but for that night he was perfect!

CHAPTER 12

I loved my new school, my new friends, and my new boyfriend. Staten Island turned out to be a wonderful place. For the first time since I was a young girl in Colombia, I was able to experience a piece of nature. The house offered an opportunity to enjoy a nearby beach and there was plenty of greenery around our neighborhood. It felt indisputably less intimidating and at the time, more formfitting than the city.

My relationship with Sam continued to escalate. We had been together for a few months and he was clear about his desire to be intimate with me, but was never forceful or impatient. He understood I had strong convictions and that I was struggling with the idea of premarital sex. With every opportunity we experimented a little more, and he had advanced to touching my breast and softly placing his hand on my private parts. In moments of passion we had expressed that we were in love with one another. Sam was not a religious person but he knew religion was important to me. To show his understanding he would say, "I am certain we will get marry one day. Josefina, God does not see two people that want to love each other as a sin." I could not help the uneasy feelings. Years of Catholic teachings about moral integrity, and Mother's explicitly expressing that keeping my virginity until marriage was virtuous, were heavily weighing on my mind. This mindset did not permit I release myself completely to my desires. Sam simply continued to woo me with his sweet affection, regard to my needs, and tolerance.

It was near the end of the summer and Dana's family was visiting from Maryland for two weeks. Among her visitors was a cousin named Megan, and she was our age. Dana was told she was to show her cousin around and, since Dana and I were together almost every day, I ended up spending much of the time with them. Inevitably I introduced her to Sam. I got the vibe she liked him but I didn't want to seem insecure or be like one of those girls who thinks everyone wants their boyfriend, so I kept it to myself. Megan was a short, hefty girl who looked at people with attitude. She was always dressed in Daisy Duke shorts, a tank top, and flip-flops. Something about her never sat well with me but I couldn't pinpoint what it was. I reminded myself that I should never judge anyone until I had good reason, and gave spending time with her a chance. Megan mentioned how she noticed I had a Spanish pronunciation. The comment was irritating. I responded abruptly, "I think you have a strong country accent. I'm from New York City and I had never heard such a distinct twang." I am certain my response irritated her as well. I could tell by her body language that the feeling of dislike was mutual. I knew I was being intolerant but I couldn't wait for her to go back to Maryland. I tried to act maturely and told myself that it was silly and childish to dislike someone I barely knew. At the time, I simply couldn't help it. She often mentioned how Staten Island was "all right" but that she loved playing with the hay and missed milking her cows. I thought it was funny she would say such a thing; she spoke of country life and I competed by bragging about city life. Oh, well! I chucked it and thought, "I guess we can't like everyone." I never meant to be mean but Dana noticed that we had a bit of a rivalry and asked me to just be nice. I valued Dana's friendship so I decided to cool it and make the best of it.

In the evenings we would normally talk, make jokes, and hang out outside and listen to music for hours. Mother called me in the house at my usual 10:00 p.m. curfew. I didn't mind my restrictions, although everyone thought it was ridiculous, but this one time I didn't want to call it a night. "Mom, please let me stay out a little longer. You know Dana's cousin is visiting from Maryland and she leaves tomorrow. We are only right outside... Please."

"Josefina, get in the house. It's late! You know better."

I felt uneasy but I did know better, and I never questioned my mom. I was raised to respect my elders, especially my parents. Period, end of discussion. I said goodnight to everyone and felt shy about kissing Sam in front of Dana and Megan, plus Mother was watching, so I just looked at him and said, "See you tomorrow Sam."

He gave me a smile and said, "Sweet dreams, say hello to your mother." His response had a fake and sarcastic tone. The way he looked at me as if to say, "Go, I don't care." It gave me an uncomfortable and unfamiliar feeling.

"Goodnight Dana. Goodnight Megan. If I don't see you tomorrow, have a safe trip back home."

Megan responded, "Yeah, alright Josefina, goodnight."

I walked away slowly, and as I went in the house I turned back and saw them laughing and joking. They were having fun and it irritated me. I walked by Mother and didn't even look at her. I was infuriated by her unreasonableness. After all, I was getting older, I was not doing anything wrong, and I was right in front of the house with a group of friends. I walked in my room and slammed the door shut. Mother did not approve of the rudeness.

She called me, "Josefina. Come over here."

"What?"

"Please come out of your room and show me you know how to quietly close the door."

Although her command made me furious, I knew if I challenged her she would punish me for being disrespectful. I walked out of my room, did not look at her, nor did I say a word. I gently grabbed the doorknob and quietly closed my bedroom door. I could hear her say, "Glad, you know how to close the doors in this house. Goodnight." That pushed me over the edge. I felt really angry, so I gestured a silent scream, and decided it was best not to respond and to just try to get some sleep.

Sam had a habit of calling me every morning. This day was different. It was midday and I just knew something was going on. I decided to call him. "Hey, I called you first! Beat you to the punch, good morning. How's it going?"

He responded, "Yeah, I've been busy, sorry."

"It's ok. What are you doing?"

"Gotta catch up with John. I'm leaving for the video store now."

"Ok, I'll see you later."

"I'll talk to you later."

The conversation was short and awkward. Later that day he came by my house. I opened the door and walked outside. We sat on the front porch as we often did, except he seemed different, quiet, and distant. I don't know why but I asked him, "Did something happen between you and Megan?"

He looked at me for what seemed like forever before he responded.

"What makes you ask me that?"

"I know you. I am sure something happened. I feel it. Tell me." I gave him an intense look.

I didn't feel like I was pressuring him too much but before I could say another word he began to cry and blurted out, "It was a stupid mistake. She was coming on to me really strong and I lost my mind for a split moment."

This was a big deal for me. I felt mixed emotions. I was angry with Sam but part of me did not want to lose him. I was confused and thought, "Ok, good people make mistakes," but I mostly felt betrayed.

"Sam, I can't be with you right now. I'm going back in the house."

"Please Josefina, I love you and I'm really sorry. I never meant for it to happen."

"It? Did you have sex?"

"I'm sorry, I couldn't help myself. She was so aggressive..." All I heard was Blah, blah, blah...

"You know what? Typical! I think you're just like every other man on the planet. Just do me a favor and leave me alone. You're disgusting!"

"Josefina, please don't say that to me! I'm really ashamed! I love you! I don't want to be without you!"

As he came toward me, I held my hand out and stopped him from trying to hold me. He was visibly upset, but I wanted to punish him for hurting me.

My eyes filled with tears as I said, "Just leave me alone! Goodbye." I repeated several times, "You're like every other guy." Without giving him the opportunity to say another word, I went back in the house.

He began an aggressive "Get Josefina back" campaign. He spoke to anyone who would lend him an ear about how sorry he was and how much he loved me. He called my house a couple of times a day, every day. He promised never to fail me again and swore he would never make that mistake again. He assured me that he never wanted to be with that girl or any other girl. His betrayal changed me in an unexpected way. I could not understand myself. I wanted to be his girlfriend more than ever, as if I found a new appreciation for his companionship. Nevertheless, I was a proud girl above all, and decided to hold back for a while. I stayed away from him while Dana and I remained good friends. I never blamed her for her cousin Megan's conduct. Dana was embarrassed and had expressed not wanting to be associated with her cousin's behavior.

"Josefina, I guess you felt something I could not see. You were right not to like her but I don't want you to be upset with me."

"Dana, I'm not upset with you. You are my closest friend."

Our relationship did not change; I knew Dana was a loyal friend and I loved her.

Sam used Dana to send me love messages and I believed he was being sincere. After all, if he were interested in Dana's cousin, he would not be communicating through her.

I felt sad during the few days I spent away from Sam. He had become someone I looked forward to seeing and talking to. I missed him. He never tired in his demonstration of affection toward me and regret for his mistake. Eventually, I decided to get back with him. I forgave him and believed him when he swore he would never hurt me again. Sadly for him, neither one of us could have predicted that it would be me who would break his heart in the end. At this stage, I felt a new appreciation for our relationship and wanted to make him happy. It seemed unlikely, but at the time overcoming his mistake with Megan had actually made us a stronger couple.

It was a significant turning point in our relationship for me. Up until the breakup, we had experienced some intense kissing sessions that had led to peeking at one another's body. Now that we had overcome the infidelity incident, I felt it was important that he got what he needed from me only. At this point, I felt ready to put all my rigid ideas about virginity aside and wanted more intimacy. We had been together over eight months. My sophomore year was half way over and I felt ready to go to the next level of closeness with him. My raging hormones were getting the best of me and I felt an urge to be completely intimate but it was accompanied by an inexplicable need to wait until my sixteenth birthday. Sam had been patient and wanted things to go smoothly so he agreed to wait.

CHAPTER 13

Sam had relentlessly talked to John, his boss who was also his friend, about me. He wanted all of us to officially meet. On my sixteenth birthday Sam planned dinner and a movie, having John and his wife, Emily joins us. It was my birthday so Mother allowed me to go without Gabriel or Dana. John and Emily were fun and treated me like an adult; we joked and laughed, and had a great time together. Sam and I were completely back to normal, and I felt happy that we were a couple again. After the double date, he took me home where my parents were waiting with a birthday cake, and everyone sang Happy Birthday. Sam, my family, and I stood in the kitchen while we ate cake and talked about my plans now that I was getting older. We laughed about stories of me when I was a little girl. I didn't mind being the subject of funny stories while we all talked for a brief while. Everything was perfect.

Sam waited until my family walked out of the kitchen and noticed my parents had turned on the TV in their bedroom before asking me to go downstairs to the basement. He needed to speak to me privately. I had excitedly looked forward to being alone with him. I walked to my room as an excuse to confirm that my parents were watching television. I walked back to the kitchen and quietly opened the door that led to the basement. He held my hand as we silently tip toed down the steps. The damp, cold place was a perfect hideaway. He placed a beautiful necklace with a gold heart charm in my hand. It was the first time a boy had ever given me anything.

After I looked at my beautiful gift, he gently took it from my hand and gestured to put it on my neck. His hands on my chest made me quiver. It was hot! He desired me and I desired him. The passion in his eyes gave me a tingling sensation from my hands to the pit of my stomach for days to come. He held my hand and pressed himself close to me, and I felt a bulge in between my legs. The passion was intense. I melted; I surrendered fearlessly. We fit so perfectly. I lost myself in a basement, which had magically transformed into the most romantic place. I wanted him desperately. We were no longer concerned that my parents watched TV only a floor above us, we just allowed the moment to take over. He pulled my panties down, put his hands under me and lifted me, commanding his body into mine. I held his back as I felt the strong thrust into my opened legs. My breathing accelerated as my nipples grew aroused by the flicking of his wet tongue. We pushed into one another as if we couldn't get enough. It was wonderful. After it was over, I pulled myself together and sneaked him out of the house. I went back to my bedroom and dreamed about what had happened. From that point forward, I wanted it as often as he could give it to me. It felt wild and I loved it.

Sam rode motor cross bikes as a hobby. He invited me to go riding with him, John, and his wife, Emily. It was a day-trip to a dirt road in Perth Amboy, New Jersey. Mother immediately denied me permission. She had seen John and Emily from afar and only knew they were a couple with two small children who lived around the block in the corner lot house. She considered biking a dangerous activity, and having never met Sam's friends was enough for her to view them as untrustworthy.

John and Emily were a young, high-spirited couple in their late twenties. Sam told me John owned a trailer and a couple of dirt bikes. They planned the day trip to a place with dirt roads and hills that were perfect for riding. Sam told Mother, "My friend, who is also my boss, and his wife are really awesome people. I know you'll like them. I'll tell them to come over so you can meet them."

Mother smiled politely and responded, "Sam, I'm sorry. I don't like bikes. They are dangerous."

He looked at me and said, "I can put my bike on their trailer and we can go to Perth Amboy together. C'mon, you'll get a chance to check out how cool it is and you'll get to do stuff with my friends." Sam thought my parents might allow me to go if I showed enthusiasm. He focused his attention on Mother again and said, "Gabriel is invited."

Mother looked at me and stated, "No," and as I predicted, my parents did not allow me to go. Even Sam's suggestion that they allow Gabriel to accompany me was not acceptable.

The continued strict denials to most permission requests did not discouraged Sam. Despite my parents' unwavering sternness, he stayed close to me in his free time and easily accepted sharing most of our plans with Dana. The three of us went to neighborhood parties, the movies, and shopped at the local flea market. Dana and I were popular girls and we participated in numerous school events without Sam, but for the most part we were the awesome threesome.

My junior year of high school had begun and it was the start of autumn. Sam and I were sitting with Baby on the porch, constantly plotting on how we could have alone time. We'd take advantage of every opportunity to have sex. It was thrilling, and we couldn't get enough of each other. Everything was great until Sam unexpectedly asked, "What does your father really do for a living?" I definitely was not prepared for the question and I instinctively became distrustful of his inquiry. "He's a business person."

Sam smirked and responded, "What business is he in?"

I was annoyed and answered, "I told you he owns a camera shop in Queens. If you don't believe me, why don't you ask him?"

Sam laughed loudly. "Why are you getting defensive about your father's business? Don't you ever wonder if he's telling you the truth? Do you ask him?"

At this point I thought maybe he knew something more than he was letting on. Feeling aggravated by his persistent curiosity, I abruptly responded, "If you have something to say, why don't you just say it?"

"WOW! I'm just wondering. Why are you getting angry?"

"I'm not angry, I'm tired. I have so much homework. I better go."

"Wait, don't leave. I'm sorry if I offended you. John and I were talking and we're interested in starting a new business and thought your dad might be willing to talk to us."

"Listen, I'm tired so I'll talk to you tomorrow."

In the past Sam had mentioned that the video store was only a front. He had given me the impression that John was involved in illegal activities. Sam didn't judge John's involvement in shady business. Instead, he felt curious and liked being around him. Sam dreamed of becoming rich while he was young, so I suspected he approved of the way John earned a living, but we had never talked about it openly. The way Sam inquired about Father led me to think he was scheming a way to conduct negotiations that could potentially connect John's underworld business with Father. I had no interest in complicating my world with darkness. I wanted to live a normal life; I preferred ignoring all that had to do with Father's business.

Sam spoke about John and his wife all the time. He mentioned that

John did not like any attention on himself or his business. He kept a low profile, but everyone who knew them personally witnessed their extravagant lifestyle. It was apparent that they had an unusually high amount of money for being the owners of a video store whose business had little to no sales. I considered John's house enormous. I had seen it from the outside and had admired the double lot with the long driveway. He parked a couple of luxury sports cars and sports utility vehicles on his oversized driveway. His cars, his house, his beautiful wife and adorable kids were enviable. They were young, fun, good looking, and rich. I found myself liking their fairytale life. Thinking that I could actually get a life like theirs with Sam was frightening and exhilarating at the same time. I struggled with inner questions regarding Sam's new interest in my father but I somehow managed to minimize and eventually dismissed all my concerns. I didn't want to lose Sam's love and friendship, as he had become an important person in my life.

There were moments when New York City seemed like a very faraway place. This city girl had changed her altar girl outfit for premarital sex and a world of possibilities that demanded a different mindset. Everything had been replaced by a bunch of fantasies clouding my mind. I began to believe the gray areas and shortcuts to making money might be acceptable.

The next day Sam visited me and I acted as if I didn't have a care in the world. This time he said, "John is outside. Come say hello." It was so unexpected and I did not know how to respond, so naturally I went outside and flashed a big smile.

Sam said, "John! Josefina still talks about how much fun she had the night of her birthday."

I approached John and said "Hello, so nice to see you again. How's

Emily doing?" It was the first time I had the opportunity to take a good look at him. He had black hair, a square jawline with very attractive and defined features. He was dressed in blue jeans and a fitted t-shirt, making it obvious he was in good shape. He had a charming smile and welcoming brown eyes.

He responded, "Nice to see you too. I agree, we had a lot of fun that night."

I looked at Sam and asked, "So, what are you guys up to?"

To my surprise, John responded, "Sam wants me to meet your dad. Would you introduce him to me?"

I responded, "Sure, why wouldn't I?" but something about the conversation was throwing me off. I started to think that beneath this charismatic facade, there was a man with two sides. There was a high level of confidence that could be mistaken for aggressiveness if put in certain circumstances. The idea of introducing him to my father made me nervous. I didn't want anyone to really know what my dad did for a living. Sam and I had a true connection, but I felt uncomfortable about the possibility of this new affiliation between John and Father. I had not thought about Father's occupation since that summer years earlier. I suspected he had not changed careers, and was troubled and confused by Sam's course of action. I wanted the finer things in life as much as Sam did, but I would never want to do anything to compromise Father. That evening I was upset and angry with Sam. I did not think of my father as an outlaw, I saw him as a man who had made some mistakes but had a good heart. Sam knew this was difficult for me, so in that moment he took a few steps back and decided not to continue to press the issue.

A few days later, Sam came by as he routinely visited. He noticed Father was home and approached him with some small talk. After a few minutes he mentioned that John, his boss, was a successful businessman and a good friend who dealt in many business ventures. My dad mentioned he had seen him in passing around the neighborhood. Before I knew it, they began talking about setting up a meeting so they could all get together and talk. This time I didn't feel the pressure of setting up the meeting. Contrary to my previous outlook, listening to this conversation was oddly pleasing. I suppose I was young and impressionable because the thought of Father relating to a successful and influential man who offered an opportunity for our family to earn a better lifestyle was becoming a bit acceptable.

Father and Mother's earnings provided us with average means. We had a nicely decorated home but we didn't enjoy extravagant trips, drive luxurious cars, or wear fashionable clothes. I had grown up experiencing being called down to the school office several times during the school year because of past due tuition payments. There had been clear indications that my parents were struggling. Mother worked long hours and I thought it would be nice if she could take a break and enjoy some free time. The possibility of being part of a lavish group of people who traveled at will and shopped excessively at high-end stores was enticing.

Later that afternoon Sam and John stopped by again. This time they both got out of the car and went up the three steps to our front door. The doorbell rang as I was listening to music loudly in my room, so I did not hear the ring. After the song was over, I heard voices in the living room so I shut the radio off and heard Sam introduce John to Father. I waited about five minutes, hoping they would leave. I could hear the low-tone voices but could not make out what the conversation was about. I thought about staying in my room, but instead I walked out into the living room area.

In a low tone I said, "Hey guys."

Sam looked at me excitedly as if he had just accomplished something important. "Hey Josefina, we wanted to stop by to say hello to Octavio."

"Ok, hi John."

"Hello Josefina. Alright Octavio, I will call you later and we can talk some more."

"Yes, we'll talk later. Good to meet you." Father did not make any comments to me about their conversation, as if meeting my boyfriend's boss was completely natural.

"Are you hungry? Dinner is ready. Your mother will be home soon, Josefina, so go ahead and set the table."

I didn't make any comment either. Everything that was happening was uncomfortable, weird, and not my business. I felt awful, but without saying a word I went over to where Mother kept the tablemats and began to set the table.

That evening I could hear my parents talking in their room. I recall Mother saying, "Octavio I think it's a terrible idea. He's our neighbor and you don't know him. This could be trouble... You should stay away from him." She repeated, "We don't know him!" Father responded in a low voice, so I couldn't hear a word he was saying. I pressed my ear against my bedroom wall with intense curiosity but it was pointless; I still could not hear a word. Beyond that conversation, I was unaware of any changes. Mother continued to do what she always did while Father, Sam, and John solidified their dealings as she went to work every day and ignored the entire situation.

After that initial meeting with John, Sam had countless private conversations with Father. I was around for most of it and knew the gist of what they were discussing but I was never in the middle of their negotiations. I grew strangely accustomed to their relationship, never giving the significance of it all much thought. Sam was in and out of my house, sometimes to visit me and sometimes to see Father. It was all set up in a natural environment. I had heard of people who were involved in such dealings as being gangster and carrying weapons, but this was not the case as I experienced it. The absence of an obvious criminal element made it all even more acceptable, almost natural. I sort of believed it was a business like any other.

Everyone in our house played his or her assigned roles without a glitch. Mother worked in the city and was only home late in the evenings and on the weekends. Gabriel and I were busy with school and extracurricular activities. Gabriel played sports and had a busy social life. I was on the track team and spent my spare time with Sam and Dana. Father was the perfect homemaker; he drove us around, made dinner almost every night, and remained a very loving parent. I appreciated the way Father took care of us, making it impossible to judge his dealings. We were a typical family with a not-so-easy-to-overlook small discrepancy.

CHAPTER 14

A year had passed since Father and John made a connection. Everything seemed to be going well and I didn't pay much mind to any of it. I felt like a regular teenager who just happened to be in a circle with a few drug dealers.

Sam and I often hung out with John and Emily. I was captivated by the way they all spent money. We enjoyed the many fun road trips, particularly the weekend beach plans. It was nice to have the freedom Father was giving me to spend time with his business associates. At home, however, I never noticed much change. I thought it strange that our financial situation seemed stagnant while my friends seemed to be doing extraordinarily well.

John's double corner lot was the largest in the neighborhood. The luxury vehicles and the motorbikes with trailers displayed on John's driveway were available for Sam to use at will. I didn't like to arbitrarily use anyone's belongings so I refused to accept such liberties, and Sam didn't want to borrow them either. He wanted it to be his. He coveted what John had and I could feel his desire for these things. John and Emily enjoyed living life to the fullest. They catered a traditional and legendary barbecue / block party every Fourth of July, complete with a mind-blowing fireworks show. The display was grand and everyone in the neighborhood was invited. I was mesmerized, as they had become influential in my life.

I was the youngest in the group and I did not have autonomy. In the beginning I needed permission to do many of the things we did together. It didn't matter to John and Emily. They loved having me around so they didn't mind asking Mother for permission. Mother must have felt obligated because of the relationship John had with Father, so soon enough she allowed me to make plans with John, Emily and Sam almost every weekend. Emily had a nanny who was always around to take care of their kids. My parents allowed me to go on many trips, including one that involved traveling by plane to Disney World in Orlando, Florida. Originally, Mother had denied me permission to travel to Orlando with the group. Sam knew that John could convince Father, the authority in our house, to give me permission, so John and Sam visited Father in reference to the business, and took advantage of the opportunity to ask if I could join them on a trip to Orlando. Father agreed to grant permission as long as Gabriel could go along. John agreed to the condition, and we all went to Orlando.

Sam and I had taken advantage of the situation to gain freedom. I must admit, for this trip I regretted being so sneaky. It was not fun! I witnessed several of John's mood swings. The worst I can recall was when Emily made him an ice cream sundae. I had normally felt intimidated by him but this scared me. I could still hear his loud voice, see his intimidating look, and feel his aggressive attitude as he approached Emily and asked, "Why didn't you put chocolate instead of caramel on the sundae? You can't even make an ice cream sundae! This is garbage!" He walked a couple of steps away from Emily and, as if he could not control his anger, he took the bowl of ice cream and swung it across the room, hitting Emily on the face. I was embarrassed and sorry for her. The kids witnessed in utter silence as she quietly apologized and cleaned up his mess. From that point forward, the vacation proceeded to go downhill. They did not bring the kids' nanny along on this trip so I ended up taking care of the kids the entire time. I loved the kids but I did not want the job. I was young and felt heavily burdened by the entire experience. I returned home tired and wanting to distance myself from the whole group. I hated being in the middle of such a volatile situation without the ability to go home, and now the delight of their company had lost its appeal.

Sam and I had spent way too much time together. I had allowed the relationship to grow too intense and felt overwhelmed by the commitment. Going to bed and waking up to Sam's company for a week in Orlando was a reality check for me. I felt I needed to take a break. My feelings of excitement and passion had dissipated. In the beginning, I took advantage of Father's negotiations to attain freedom but after the week in Florida I began to feel like a sold slave, as if I was being used like a bargaining chip. I knew Sam was responsible for my position and I began to resent him for it. I felt at the mercy of the fragile relationship between Father and John, and it slowly began to take a toll on me.

Sam knew he could manipulate my parents. Whenever he wanted me to go somewhere he would claim it was John's request. In the past we had chuckled over how Sam used it to our advantage, and we thought it was funny that Father never denied a "John request". Now I felt everything was distorted. I had a new viewpoint since the experience in Orlando; it had made everything different. It all went from new and exciting to obligated and dreadful. During that week I had been in the middle of many uncomfortable incidents. I witnessed John's outburst at Sam as friction grew between them. Sam apparently had been pushing for equality in how the profits were split and John did not approve. I heard Sam argue that he considered himself the main risk taker and thought he deserved a bigger piece of the pie. After we got back to New York it seemed like their differences worsened. Their companionships began to feel tense, awkward, forced… I felt that being part of this group of pretenders had become a nightmare.

It took Mother a long while but she began to notice that Sam had a strong grip on me and she did not like it. She began to complain about the long commute into New York for work and spoke about her interest in moving to a town in New Jersey. I knew her desire to move was mainly because she wanted to put distance between Sam and me. My distress had reached a high point and she detected my obvious discomfort, showing concern for having been absent for most of it. I assumed she lacked the courage to impose her wishes on Father.

Instead of quarreling with Father, she strategically suggested we visit a small town in New Jersey. "Octavio, it would be an easier commute into the city for work. I feel tired and I don't spend much time with the kids. Let's just go and visit. Maybe you'll like it." Father was not a complicated person and agreed to visit the town Mother suggested. We drove around and unanimously expressed how much we liked the quaint small town.

The location had the great Main Street, USA appeal. It had several small shops and a railroad station in the center of town. The place looked wholesome, with a fairly close commute into New York and, most importantly, it distanced us from Sam and John. I agreed that it seemed like the perfect place to move to because I had grown intolerant to Sam. I thought it was a good change for us. Although I loved my school and it was my senior year of high school, I wanted to disassociate myself from the relationship with the people in Staten Island. I didn't mind trading my school for a chance to get away from all the stress. We found a nice house and, while in the process of closing the deal, I had to repeatedly reminded myself that I had to be patient, that finding the right home was a time consuming process. In the meantime, Mother silently kept an eye on me as I continued to be part of the complicated web.

Sam knocked on the door of my house. I opened the door and said, "Hi."

We kissed and he said, "Josefina, where's your dad? I need to see him."

"He's in his bedroom. The door is closed so just knock. Let him know you're here." He went into my parents' bedroom and spoke to my dad in private.

After a brief moment, Sam came out with a black bag wrapped into a square-like shape under his armpit. He said, "C'mon, let's go."

I replied, "Where?" By now my parents had allowed me the freedom to leave the house at will with Sam.

"I have to run an errand for your dad. He said you're allowed to come with me."

"He did? I have some homework."

Sam gave me a look I perceived meant I had no choice. "It'll be quick. You can finish your homework later."

I responded, "Ok, hold on and let me get my jacket."

We got into Sam's new car. Sam believed he was achieving his financial dreams. He had stacks of hundred dollar bills piled on his night table, and paid most of the bills in his mother's house, but I felt a deep dissatisfaction. I never envisioned I would ever voluntarily or involuntarily get involved in these dealing. I felt uneasy in his car. We had never done such a run before, and as Sam drove on, I was becoming increasingly uncomfortable. I was telling him that I hoped we weren't planning to meet any menacing people as I noticed he focused his attention on the rearview mirror. He'd noticed a patrol car behind us and jokingly mentioned the police presence to me. He seemed unfazed. "There's a police car behind us, you better behave,"

As he laughed, I felt a POW! Kick in the face. My stomach was in knots. I looked at Sam and it dawned on me that we were a pair of inexperienced kids playing a dangerous game. My blood pressure dropped at the thought of getting pulled over in possession of this illegal merchandise in the car. I held Sam's hand nervously. He told me to relax, that everything would be fine.

We stopped at the red light as the police cruiser drove next to us and waited to turn. I could see in my peripheral vision that the police officer behind the wheel looked our way for a long moment. I made no eye contact to avoid any sign of my hidden discomposure. In my head I heard a deafening scream, "Please, no! I'm sorry, I didn't know what I was doing," but instead I looked forward.

Out of the corner of my eye, I had a side vision of the police car turning right onto the crossroad, and couldn't help the outburst of uncontrollable weeping. Sam refused to pull over, and seemed annoyed as he asked, "What's wrong with you? Sorry I mentioned the police car to you, I was just kidding." I did not answer, so he continued, "I told you it's OK! Get yourself together." I could tell he was getting upset because I did not calm down. He continued, "Stop crying! Let's do this and go home!"

I thought of all the "what ifs". At the time there had been some issues with racial profiling by police officers, so I wondered... What if we weren't a couple of white kids in a car? What if we looked like typical thugs? What if we had a broken taillight and were pulled over for unrelated reasons? What if I had to face a jail sentence? My life would be ruined!

It was clear to me that I had made a terrible mistake. Sam, the person I felt comfortable with, the person I had so much in comm with and felt I loved, was a distant memory. The Sam I truste looked forward to talking to every day was gone. The attr gone. I didn't know if it was a temporary feeling, but I couldn't think past the moment.

We arrived at the destination. He agreed to let me wait in the car while he met the contacts. I felt an urge to use the bathroom but held my composure. After a few minutes he came back, got in the car, and we took off. We were quiet for most of the drive back home. I could tell there was a stack of money in the bag he placed on the center compartment. I didn't ask any questions or make any comments. He was unaffected by the danger of it all and seemed frustrated by my silence. I now understood just how different we were. I was perturbed and couldn't wait to get home and away from his presence.

Before I got out of his car I said, "Sam, I will never be in a car with you or anyone else and drugs again. Never! I really think you need to rethink your choices. You need to quit this all together."

"Josefina, you are over reacting. That was nothing. Besides, I was teasing you about the cops. He wasn't going to stop us."

I gave him an unpleasant look and walked in the house.

I didn't share the eye opening experience with anyone at home. My mother seemed tired, disconnected, and clouded. She worked long hours and spent much of her time traveling back and forth between New York City and Staten Island. She had been conditioned to believe my father's business was no different than the work ━━ ━━gers had done during the prohibition era. Alcohol had lost its ━━ ━━t since it was legalized for sale and consumption ━━ ━━" of drugs would probably have the same ━━lized. It had become a culturally accepted ━━y, she seemed to still love Father. She ━━ved the anxiety of trying to raise kids alone while working long hours and living in a neighborhood that was rapidly changing. In her sincere effort to raise Gabriel and me in a "normal" family setting, she neglected to acknowledge the wolf in grandma's house.

Gabriel was involved in sports and always busy. He too had established a social life. He had many friends and frequently attended school and neighborhood gatherings. He really didn't know the details of Sam and Father's dealings, and I chose to keep him in the dark about my distress. I was ashamed of the person I was being. I felt that as long as Gabriel remained unaware, I could still preserve the innocence and joy of my past.

My faith and my religious beliefs would continue to be challenged. I had made choices that would mark me with guilt and shame for many years to come. In Washington Heights it was easy to recognize the criminal element. It sometimes wore a mask and carried a gun, and everyone knew to stay away from it. In Staten Island I began to believe that friendships were used to disguise predatory evil and to lure the innocent, the vulnerable, the exposed. In my mind, I dramatized drugs as the wickedness that presented itself, wrapped in a luxurious package. I believed it only disclosed its dangerous, bitter substances after it was opened. Sam had fallen from grace. To me, he personified the old proverb, "Not everything that glitters is gold." Today, I realize Sam did not initially set out to exploit his intimate knowledge of me. I believe he was simply reckless and greedy. At the time I doubted his intentions and began to see him as an adversary.

CHAPTER 15

Father was too close to the situation to acknowledge what was happening to me. It was his business and he did not see anything wrong with it. He had come from a line of men who had been involved in bootlegging and were open to any business that proved profitable. Father had shared stories about the poverty in Colombia, and he was familiar with the café culture. The coffee growers in Colombia's tropical zona cafetera worked the fincas and earned pennies for their crop. I listened to many stories of unfair treatment and exploitation. For many landowners, cultivating coca leafs was a way of rising above poverty since it was a much more profitable crop. It was seen as a blessing for Colombia's agricultural industry because it provided farmers the opportunity to finally earn a good wage. Father explained the reason the United States identified Colombia with the cocaine trade was because, although Peru and Bolivia dominated the coca-leaf production, their crop was sent to the jungle labs in southern Colombia where the cartels dominated the production of cocaine. Father hated the cartels and the rebel groups' violence.

I was curious about why Peru and Bolivia had to export the crop to Colombia, so I looked for information and found an article somewhere about the process of converting the coca leaf into cocaine. It completely blew my mind! I couldn't believe the amount of harsh chemicals involved in the process. It was crazy! I thought anyone who used the substance should probably die instantaneously. I read that it begins by soaking the leaf in gasoline inside metal drums. When it converts to alkaloid, the producers drain and filter the substance into barrels with diluted acid. Then they remove the gasoline from the acid layer and proceed to add sodium bicarbonate or ammonia to the solution. This process makes the cocaine base, which is then filtered through the use of a cloth. The remaining substance is dried, resulting in a purer form of cocaine base. The cocaine base is then dissolved in ethyl acetate, acetone, or ether, where it's heated in a hot water bath called a "baño maría." At that point methyl ethyl ketone is added to the boiling liquid, along with concentrated hydrochloric acid. The process results in the crystallization of cocaine hydrochloride. The excess solvents are removed first by hand, and then by using a hydraulic press. All solvents are finally removed using microwave ovens, thereby creating the basis for powder cocaine.

After learning that information, I thought the solution to the trafficking problem was easy. If the government was truly interested in placing a halt to the cocaine trade in the United States, all it needed to do was create a law that would prohibit and penalize any company that produced such chemicals from exporting their product to Colombia, Peru, Bolivia, Brazil, or any other country with the soil to grow the coca leaf.

I shared my thoughts with Father and he laughed, "Josefina, you're a smart girl but what would the DEA, FBI, Customs, and other law enforcement agencies do if the business of illegal activities came to a complete stop? They need their jobs honey, that is why nothing is ever so simple." Father was partially amused by my naïve observation and not insulted that I was speaking about a business he was involved in.

Father was a great storyteller. He told stories that he had heard from people he knew. "Josefina, the mountains and jungle areas where the coca crops grow are controlled by the Revolutionary Armed Forces of Colombia. They are known as La FARC." He would say, "Esos hiweputas controlan el narcotráfico y son malos como ellos solos!"

(Those sons of bitches control the narcotrafficking and they are evil like no other.)

La FARC actively expanded by continuously purchasing land for the purpose of cultivating the coca leaf. Eventually, Colombia replaced Peru and Bolivia as primary producers of coca, and became responsible for the highest cocaine production in the world. It was impossible to stop a business that was believed to employ an astounding number of households in the region. Father was the only one of five brothers who lived in the United States, and had become a low level liaison between a few buyers and suppliers. He became involved through my uncles, like most Colombians. At first, Father's brothers viewed cocaine trafficking as an opportunity to remedy the increasing poverty and the deteriorating conditions for the working farmers. No one understood the darkness it brought to all in its path. No one could have foreseen the violence and greed that would sweep the nation like a plague without a cure.

I remembered during our short time in Colombia, Father had taken us to his brother's cattle ranch. We watched my uncle milk a cow and we even drank the milk while it was still warm. La finca had an Olympic size pool. Unlike the farmers that worked the coca fields, my uncle did not have any financial struggles. He had plenty of cattle, luscious mango trees, and countless tropical fruit crops. He was a wealthy, well-liked man who, like my father, was married but loved many women. His wife apparently did not mind that he had fathered many bastard children, and remained his wife until the day he died. It was said that at his funeral there were at least eight women with countless children who claimed to be his heirs. His wife didn't find such claims amusing and did not hesitate to arm herself and her daughters with rifles and threaten to kill anyone who dared touch their possessions. My uncle's rightful family was made up of his wife and three daughters, and none of them ever held his ill behavior against him. Instead, they admired his manhood because he was a good provider. I understood my uncle was involved and involved his brothers in the business simply because it was very profitable and because it gave him a powerful social status. He was loved by many people in Barranquilla and to this day is regarded affectionately.

That night in Sam's car, I clearly comprehended that my indirect involvement in this business would have direct consequences if I continued to participate in any way. I was afraid to tell Father what had happened in the car with Sam. I knew he might dismiss it as a minor thing but I felt in my heart that my luck could run out and I began to feel guilty. I remembered the immense love I felt for God, I remembered the pride I felt when I served my church, and I remembered I was a stupid kid. Thoughts rushed into my head, the values I lived by were obscured by an enticing idea of a life with insignificant material things. I had felt pride to show off the finer things in our home, like the decorative pieces in our living room and the new furniture that adorned our home. I was filled with nonsense that had evolved into complicated contradictions which I had difficulty processing. I remembered that I did not mind the picked-up couch from a nearby dumpster in Washington Heights. I wanted good food, clean clothes. I wanted my school tuition paid on time! I wanted to be a real kid, without the hassle of a situation that had gotten out of hand. In that car with Sam I felt sick. I had a headache and a stomachache. When will it stop? Who was I turning into? When was I going to stand up for myself, against myself? I didn't remember at what point I had become the accomplice of a drug dealer. I tortured myself over the question: Why was I betraying myself?

I spent days thinking about the incident and realized I was in over my head but there was nothing I could do. I felt obligated to the situation because I had unwillingly served as a liaison between Father, Sam, and John. I remembered that a woman who worked hard for her earnings and rejected the lifestyle raised me. Mother weighed heavily on me that night; she was my conscious. I knew my moral compass needed calibration and I viewed her as an exemplary woman. Mother had never shared her feelings about Father's occupation with me but her actions spoke volumes. She never missed a day of work and she demanded Gabriel and I prioritize our education. She was an enigma; strict yet permissive, ignorant yet wise; righteous yet corrupt. She was a walking contradiction. She allowed corruption to infiltrate that which she protected most and held dearest to her heart. I thought Mother was numbed or asleep, and wanted to shake her until she'd awaken but I couldn't because of guilt and shame.

Negative thoughts often kept me awake at night. Several weeks later I was feeling particularly restless. I needed to get some sleep but visions of a simpler life in Washington Heights kept me awake. I missed the days of being carefree. I missed the water balloon fights with Gabriel. I missed running away from Baby so she would not scratch my feet. I wanted the impossible; to go back in time. All I could do for now was try to get some sleep. I decided to get up and use the bathroom, hoping it would ease my restlessness. I quietly walked out of my bedroom and noticed the television was on in Gabriel's room. I opened his door carefully and noticed he was not asleep. I felt safe in his room so I decided to walk in. He looked at me and asked, "Josefina, are you ok?"

"No. I've been having trouble falling asleep lately."

"Ok, watch TV with me for a while, if you want."

"Yeah, I might as well."

"Josefina?"

"Yes Gabriel."

"Something sort of funny happened to me at school today."

"Oh yeah, what was it?"

"The gym teacher got angry because I wouldn't give up the basketball."

"What did you do?"

"I told him he couldn't have the basketball because I was still playing. He didn't take it lightly."

"So what happened?"

"You know how priests are, he thought he could hit me. I told him, first he'd have to catch me and I took off running. I ran as fast as I could from the basketball court on the outside grounds into the school building. I looked back to see if he was catching up and I could see his beet red face and a thread of veins around his forehead. He looked like he was ready to poop his pants, ha ha ha!"

"Oh my god! Gabriel, are you kidding?"

"NO! I'm not. I knew if he caught me he would probably kill me, so I ran into the school office. I noticed the principal's door was wide open, and ran into his office and noticed no one was inside. But I heard the gym teacher scream my name. He said, 'Mr. Lopez, you're in big trouble.' I was so scared I locked myself in the Principal's office."

I was in complete disbelief, "Gabriel, you must be making this up!"

"I swear the whole story is true. The principal, the gym teacher, the principal's secretary, the school's guidance counselor, they were all pounding on the door. 'Open this door at once Mr. Lopez!'"

Gabriel could barely get the words out. He was laughing so much he had tears in his eyes. I was too stunned to say a word. My jaw dropped and I was sitting there with my mouth wide open for about ten seconds. I finally lowered the volume on the TV, turned on his lamplight and asked, "So what happened?"

He looked at me but did not respond fast enough. I was annoyed. I rolled my eyes, smirk, and asked him, "Did you just make up this whole story?"

He looked at me as his voice cracked. "No way! It's all true…"

He got up off his bed and continued, "Josefina, everyone was screaming as I demanded they call Dad."

"Seriously?"

"Yeah, seriously! The old man always has our back. You know that."

I stayed completely silent, feeling the irony of his statement. Gabriel continued, "So they claimed they would call him after I opened the door but I knew better. I picked up the principal's phone and called the house."

"Gabriel! This story keeps getting crazier!"

"I know! Hahahah! So, Dad picks up the phone and says, 'Hola,' and I immediately said, 'Dad, the gym teacher is going to kill me! You have to come to the school now.'"

"Josefina, I couldn't believe it. He asked no questions, he simply told me he was on his way to my school and hung up the phone. I could tell he slammed it abruptly because I could hear a tremendously loud bang as the call got disconnected."

"Oh my god! Gabriel, so what happened?"

"Dad must have taken a private jet to my school. I swear it must have been two minutes later and I could hear his deep melodic voice, 'Son, open the door.' I felt so relieved; he was there quicker than I imagined. I immediately unlocked the door, and as soon as Dad walked in the room, everyone's tone changed. They were ready to speak to me calmly."

"This only happens to you! Gabriel, you're the best!"

"No, Dad is the best. I told him the gym teacher threatened to hit me and chased me all the way into the building. I told everyone I was scared and running to get the principal's help but he wasn't in his office."

"So… What did Dad do?"

"Dad asked, 'Who wants to hit my son?'"

"I quickly pointed at the gym teacher and said, 'He does!' This is probably the funniest part. Dad rolled up his sleeves, took off his watch and as he made a fist said, 'You want to hit my son? Hit me! I got something for you!' The principal stepped in and asked him to settle down. At that point I did everything in my power not to crack up."

I was incredibly amused by the story and some of the negative feelings I had toward Father diminished a bit. I loved Gabriel and was glad he was there to protect him. I laughed until my belly hurt, "Gabriel this story is awesome! So what happened in the end?"

"In the end, they explained that I had broken multiple school disciplinary rules and that I was to be suspended. Dad responded that he should sue the gym teacher for abuse of power. The principal wanted to diffuse the situation so, after a lot of back and forth arguing, he agreed not to suspend me and to let the incident go with a warning. Dad agreed he would speak to me about consequences but the minute we stepped out of the school building, he told me not to ever let any of those abusive bastards lay a hand on me. He gave me a hug and told me I had done the right thing."

"Yeah Gabriel, Dad is good about stuff like that. He is so funny!"

"He's the best! Love the old guy!"

At this point I felt much more relaxed. Gabriel and I laughed and talked for about an hour, then I walked back to my room and easily dozed off.

CHAPTER 16

John expressed concerns about the business. Sam's demands for equal sharing in the profits had placed much strain on their relationship. John was not going to "allow a young punk to ruin his life." He openly expressed the fact that he already had so much money, a gorgeous home, a stunning wife and a perfect family, he did not need the aggravation from an immature, overly ambitious, weak, and confused boy. John was troubled by Sam's overzealous attitude about money and his insolence. He believed working with Sam had become a risky and volatile situation. John also knew that Father was an old man with no backup; he could get away with stiffing Father if he chose to. He constantly threatened not to pay if Sam refused to follow the original set up. Sam did not cooperate. His fearlessness and inexperience was becoming trouble for all involved. At first, John decided to lessen the amount of merchandise he accepted and eventually discontinued all negotiations with Sam and Father.

The partnership would dissolve, ending the days when everyone had a steady flow of money. John had the upper hand and was able to pull the plug at will. Sam's disadvantage was that he was financially struggling. He was carrying the financial burdens at his mother's house and needed to find a way to continue doing so. In the beginning, the business had been profitable for Father. He was paid without reluctance but now he had to harass Sam for payment. The last merchandise was almost a total loss for my father. Sam got John to pay in the long run, but at that point it was evident that the work between them was done for good.

Things continued to go south for Sam and me. I continued to grow more distant every day. I wanted to end the relationship altogether but felt stuck in a cycle of guilt, mistaken assumptions of responsibility, remorse, and a mixture of debilitating, misunderstood, defrauded ideas. He sensed my lack of interest and thought if he made more money I was ambitious enough to want him again. He misunderstood, because at that point there was nothing he could do. My feelings had changed and I no longer enjoyed his company. There was so much tension between us. I was silently relieved that I no longer had to deal with John and Emily. I lamented having stopped spending time with Dana because of my connection to Sam and their friendship. I really just missed being a regular teenage girl. Sam would argue constantly about why his dealing with Father and John were terminated. I would listen to his absurd and delusional reasoning about his right to earn just as much as everyone else and would respond that it was his desire to overstep his boundaries that terminated the dealings and that if he wasn't careful it could bring him bigger troubles.

Although it was very unpleasant between us, Sam still talked about marrying me and tried to persuade me into eloping. I did not want to continue our relationship, much less marry him. I stayed in the relationship in part because Sam manipulated my religious beliefs. He reminded me that he had taken my virginity and used guilt to keep us together. In the past, I appreciated when he stated he would marry me after high school as a way to relieve me of my sin and renew my faith, but now I could not make such a commitment to a person I knew I was no longer in love with.

A few months went by and although John and Sam remained friends, Sam was no longer working at the video store and was looking for a fresh start. His savings was running low and he needed money to continue helping out his mother. I had always encouraged Sam to go back to school, so I proposed that he at least study to take the General Educational Development (GED) exam and earn his high school equivalency diploma. He wanted to please me so he signed up to prepare for the GED. Once he completed and passed the exam, he registered at a local vocational school and attended class twice a week in the evening. Sam thought pursuing a career as an electrician was his best option since his father owned an electric service company, and I was happy he had made the decision to better himself. I hoped it would put an end to all his twisted ideas. I wanted to be away from all that darkness. I knew he was confused and needed to become stable. I felt sorry for him but I was mainly looking for the right time to break up with him.

By this time I was well into my senior year in high school. My parents had found a nice home in New Jersey and I was transferred to a local Catholic high school. I didn't mind that with my move I lost my popular status. I missed being well known and liked by many friends but my priority was to find a good college and move on with my life. Sam would have to take a road trip in order to visit me and sometimes it was difficult for him to do that during the weekdays. Gradually, things had settled down. Sam continued taking courses to get his electrician certification while I quietly planned to go away to college after graduation. I knew the greater the distance, the quicker I could separate from him. I tried to hide my intentions but every time I filled out a college admissions application, he would cry and plead with me not to leave him. I didn't know how we had reached such a pathetic point in our relationship. I had grown true disdain for him and couldn't wait to be rid of what I had started to perceive as blackmail. Every day I would wish for time to go by quickly so I could go away to college. I no longer believed marrying him would earn me God's forgiveness so I went to confession and received absolution. My faith was strong and I knew God would forgive my sins and that He would help me get away from Sam.

On one of Sam's visits to our new home in New Jersey, I noticed he had a big smile on his face and seemed unusually happy. I asked him,

"Hey Sam, what's going on?"

"Hey Josefina, I had a great day in school today."

"Really, that's nice. I'm glad to hear it. What happened?"

"I've been talking to this kid in my class. He and I have become very comfortable with one another so we started talking about all sorts of things and he mentioned that he has an interest in buying stuff from your father."

I couldn't believe my ears. I felt angry with him but I tried to calmly dissuade him. "Sam, I thought you liked school and wanted to work for your dad."

"I do. This would be a quick score. My savings is gone and I'm not working yet. I think we could really use the money. Plus, I really trust this guy. He's like me. Believe me, there's nothing to worry about with him."

I was not happy about his new connection, "Sam, would you please just forget it? You have a plan. Why do you want to mess things up?"

"I'm going to speak to your father about getting me the merchandise. I don't know how much he wants yet, but I know he is very interested."

"Sam, are you listening to me? Just stay away from it. It's trouble! You've come a long way in school. Things are looking up, just be patient."

He completely ignored my pleadings and said, "Where's your dad? I

152

need to speak to him, make sure he can do it before I confirm with this guy."

It was clear there wasn't much I could say to change his mind. He would not listen no matter how hard I tried. I knew I needed to be careful around him. I sensed his growing anxiety, so I backed off. I could tell he wanted to return to the time when he had stacks of hundred dollar bills on his night table and was covering all the expenses at his mother's house. His prime motivation was based on the mistaken assumption that making lots of money was a way of regaining my interest.

Although my father was no longer dealing with him, Sam was persistent and persuasive. I could not believe he continued to look for new buyers while attending school, and now he was about to go back to the business that I hated.

I was accustomed to existing in this unhappy relationship and had adopted the attitude that for the time being I would simply go along with it. After all, since our move to New Jersey I did not deal with Sam much. My plan to finish high school and go away to college was solid. For now, it was a matter of killing time until my graduation. □

CHAPTER 17

"Hey, I have to go see my friend from school." I gave him a confused look. He went on, "You know, the one I told you is really trustworthy." I still did not respond. "Josefina, the one who is interested in buying stuff from me, let's go. Take a ride with me."

I was hoping he had changed his mind. I stayed quiet. I thought an awkward silence might shake some sense into him. "Remember? You know, my friend from school. C'mon. Josefina! He's waiting for me."

I took a deep breath and responded, "I really don't want to go Sam, and I have things to do. Anyway, you know I'm not comfortable riding around with stuff in your car."

"I don't have anything on me. I'm just going to talk to this kid, I want to let him know what I have going on is good quality. He told me he had sold in the past and that he had tons of buyers but no merchandise. It'll be quick. Let's go, we barely ever spend time together!"

In the recent past, I had refused to cooperate with his demands. It had led to fierce arguments. A few weeks earlier we had an argument that intensified into a physical confrontation. The dispute escalated so quickly, before I knew it we were engaged in a pushing match. I remember thinking he looked so unattractive as he pushed me with all his strength. I didn't expect it, and ended up slipping and falling sideways, causing my face to hit the side of my night table. He apologized immediately, "Oh Josefina! I didn't mean it! Please, I'm sorry... I care about you so much! You're the only girl I ever want in my life. Please forgive me... I love you so much!" It all sounded like, "Blah, Blah, Blah!" to me. I knew he didn't mean for me to fall and get hurt, but I was thoroughly disgusted. I had never experienced a physically threatening situation before and it shocked me. I couldn't tell Father or Gabriel; I knew they would confront Sam. I feared it would lead to him divulging my father's dealings to people we knew in the community. I also feared him telling my parents about our intimate relationship. I did not want to make Sam an enemy so I kept it to myself. He had the upper hand and I had no choice but to accept his apology. I used make-up for a week to conceal the bruise on the side of my face. I didn't want to bring any additional trouble into the situation and thought it best to keep it a secret.

I wanted to avoid the pointless inconvenience of a fight, so I agreed to accompany him to his classmate's house. We ended up in front of a suburban home in an upper class New Jersey neighborhood. A tall, thin white man wearing a blue oxford shirt and blue jeans was hosing the front yard. I recall in great detail the events of that day. Sam parked his car on the side of the house and stepped out. I opened the passenger door, hearing a little voice whisper in my ear, "Something is not right." The way he looked at us seemed unnatural, rehearsed, peculiar... giving us an almost fake greeting. It felt indescribably confusing and awkward. The man said hello. Hesitating before making eye contact with me, he called out for his son to come outside. "Your friend Sam is here with his girlfriend, come outside!"

A clean-cut, preppy looking young man came outside. His appearance was just as bizarre as his father. He looked like the All American boy-next-door. I felt like I was in an episode of the "Leave It to Beaver" show, with a twist. He said hello and carried on a short conversation. Sam and the young man walked away, talking for a short while. I was left standing next to Sam's classmate's father. We had a brief, meaningless conversation until Sam returned. Sam and I politely said goodbye, got back in the car, and left.

During the car ride to my house, Sam expressed excitement about the plan to meet his friend before their next evening class. I could still hear him saying, "This kid is reliable and trustworthy. I know I can trust him... We are meeting in two days for an exchange."

"Sam, my prom is in two days. That's not going to be possible."

After a quiet pause, Sam continued, "I remembered that. Yes it will. I'm meeting him in the parking lot of your school."

I should have said no way! Instead, I stayed quiet. I'm not certain why I wasn't compelled to protest in that moment. The truth is, I wanted to get home and away from Sam. I was fed up with the events of the day.

My father was no longer dealing with Sam but he must have been equally desperate for this deal. As I had predicted, Sam was persuasive and determined. Father's reluctance should have been a deterrent for Sam, but it wasn't. To my surprise, Father accepted Sam's proposal for "an easy, trouble free, quick score." The agreement to conduct the transaction on a night that was supposed to be fun was unsettling to me. It put a damper on my prom night and further destroyed my relationship with Sam. His mindset was to kill two birds with one stone and arranged for the exchange to take place in the school parking lot. I could still hear Sam say, "What is the problem? It will not interfere with our fun. This is the most convenient way to do it. We'll go in the school immediately after and join the dance."

Mother always stated she prayed for a guardian angel to protect

Gabriel and me throughout our lives since the day we were born. On the night of my prom, through divine intervention or the protection of my guardian angel, Father was unable to get the merchandise. Sam was furious that the exchange would have to be rescheduled. "My friend is disappointed. He said his buyers are not happy!"

"Well that's too bad! Sam, I don't think you should go through with this." I couldn't help but feel nervous about this new connection. "Sam, I think this is a blessing. I had an overwhelming sense that something was not right since the time we met this guy and his father. I am certain I overheard the father ask in a whisper if you are the guy. I couldn't help feeling like the whole thing was staged."

I couldn't get past stereotyping the two white, upper class men as unlikely characters to be dealing cocaine. It didn't add up in my head. Sam made light of my comments about their appearance and played down what I had heard. The father's question had rubbed me the wrong way. Sam assured me the business with this new friend was not as risky because the kid was not desperate, that he simply wanted extra cash. He demanded I stop bringing negativity into the situation. I reminded Sam he was no longer dealing with trusted individuals; this was a total stranger, and it was all very frightening to me. Sam stayed determined, and there was nothing I could do to stop him. Sam went as far as claiming he blindly trusted his new friend. He arranged to move forward with the meeting as soon as the goods became available. I had no choice but to accept his decision. He managed to successfully plant doubt to my suspicions, which prompted me to disregard my instincts.

It was Sunday evening, a day after my prom, and I was reading a news article designed to create public awareness on the seriousness of the drug trafficking problem. I knew the problem was serious but the admittance that the Bush administration's anti-drug efforts were falling short was surprising. The National Institute on Drug Abuse

(NIDA) reported that there was an increase in the number of reported cocaine-related hospital emergency cases. The number of cocaine related injuries had increased, along with the number of drug deaths. It accused the Bush administration's efforts as being mostly a public relations campaign and not a priority. The most impacting part of the article for me was a quote written by former President George H.W. Bush, "America's porous borders, combined with its seemingly unquenchable thirst for drugs and the enormous profitability of drug trafficking, make this one of the toughest wars to wage... But if we're going to win this war on drugs, we have to win it on the home front. That means examining the alternatives and talking about the problem – parent to child, friend to friend, candidate to candidate."

This really hit home for me. It was as if the President was speaking to me directly. I thought of ways I could help lessen the problem, because it made me feel like a terrible citizen. I was trapped and could not figure a way out. I wondered how many people were in similar situations. Many news reports stated that, despite federal agencies such as the Drug Enforcement Agency's (DEA) continuous battle in securing our borders, it seemed like the problem continued to be on the rise. Father confused me because he spoke of the ruthlessness of the drug cartels and his awareness of Colombia's terrible crisis. He seemed to be realizing that it was time to turn away from his dealings but something kept him from completely ending that stage of his life. I suppose he had been in the business for so long that he did not know what else he would do to support our family.

Colombia's government was ready to unite forces with the United States in order to gain a handle on the problem. Colombian politicians who opposed the drug cartels were in increasing danger of becoming victims of kidnappings and public bombings. The Colombian government acknowledged the imminent danger citizens were under due to the drug epidemic and had mustered up the courage to fight the evil forces.

After reading the news article, a surge of disturbing ideas were wreaking my head like a volcanic eruption. Sickening me, turning my stomach, tingling my hands, and keeping me awake. I just kept thinking that Sam was blinded by his ambition and failed to realize that dealing in the business had become a huge risk and an awful contribution to society. I told myself that I was ready to demand that Sam stop his dealings. I would also speak to Father about ending the whole thing. I looked at the time and realized it was past midnight.

Sam said he would call after his meeting and no word yet. I was jumping out of my own skin. In a nostalgic moment I walked outside and wished for a little jasmine therapy. In the past, the floral scent had soothed and calmed me, but tonight in New Jersey, far from the floral shrubs in Staten Island, its magic was gone. I did fifty jumping jacks, hoping to tire and calm myself but it was pointless. I could not contain my restlessness so I walked back into the house and decided to call Sam's house. Unexpectedly, his mother picked up the phone. At that moment my heart sunk. She quickly confirmed that all my fears had come true, "It's done! I hope you and your father are happy! Your boyfriend is going to jail for a long time!" I hung up the phone and began to cry uncontrollably. I knew it! I was certain this moment would come. A nightmare that I wished would go away was just about to get worse. I couldn't help but think of the humiliation I would have had to endure if the arrest would have taken place at my school's parking lot. I envisioned all; my friends staring and laughing. I would have been the talk of the party, and not in a good way. I refocused on Sam and felt overwhelmingly sad. I knew his life was ruined, and I believed mine was too.

I woke my parents up and told them. They seemed disconnected.

Father said "Josefina, there's nothing you can do tonight. Try to get some sleep. We will deal with this tomorrow."

Mother was mostly quiet, only making a short statement, "I said it from the start Octavio! You should not have been dealing with Sam." I felt angry and thought my parents were merciless and didn't care about anything.

I walked back to my bedroom. I've erased the clarity of that moment out of my memories. I have a vague recollection of the events of that night and still, I can't recall my parents making any effort to console me or provide guidance in this horrible moment. My anxiety was so high, but I finally reached a point of exhaustion at five a.m. and couldn't help but fall asleep. By seven a.m. I was wide-awake. Catastrophic thoughts were rushing through my head. I didn't know how to handle the problem. I thought about the possibility of Sam serving a long sentence. Will he continue to emotionally blackmail me? The thought of owing my life to him in exchange for his not divulging his source was terrifying. I knew now it would be impossible for me to go away to college or break up with him. I felt sorry for Sam, I felt that I owed him loyalty, and even felt a little love for him again. I was angry and thought it unfair that he was caught instead of the other older men who had taught him the trade. I immediately self-corrected and realized he had made choices on his own and that I shouldn't feel disloyal toward Father.

That morning I thought about the young man from his school and his father. Could either implicate me as an accomplice? I was at their house with Sam! I had never been more scared. I needed to find out what we were up against. I wiped my tears, put my hair up in a ponytail and got dressed. I wish I could have headed to Sam's mother's house but we had moved an hour away. I called Sam's house again. At first, I didn't know what to say and, just as I expected, his mother was angry and spoke to me in a very nasty way.

"This is your father's fault! He put my son in jail!"

I reacted without thinking of the consequences of her wrath. "It's not just my father's fault! You knew he had stacks of money on his dresser. He was generous to you and your daughter. He paid the bills in your house! Did you bother to find out how a young man who worked at a video store was managing to carry such a load? Why didn't you stop him?" In that moment I thought of my own mother and how she too failed to stop Father from dealing with my boyfriend.

His mother backed off immediately. She calmly told me he would be arraigned at the Criminal Court of New Jersey by 10 a.m. She was not sure at that point what the charges were and had spent the night tirelessly researching for a criminal defense attorney. At this point, the most difficult part of the problem was dealing with the uncertainty of the situation. We were hoping he would be granted a reasonable bail but there was no way to tell yet. After the initial confrontation, his mother was surprisingly calm. I don't know if she accepted that her lack of guidance and her ignoring the situation contributed to its escalation, but I believe she had accepted responsibility for her part and quickly found enough strength to help me gain my composure. We both agreed to help Sam and not be judgmental of one another. After the sobbing subsided she calmly said to me, "Josefina, a few minutes before you phoned me I was able to get in touch with an attorney who agreed to meet me at the courthouse. Do you want to come with me?"

I responded, "Where is your daughter?"

"She could not take the time off from work. I think she's angry and doesn't want to deal with this."

I knew Sam's mother felt alone so I responded, "I'm so scared, but yes, I will go with you. I will try to help in any way I can."

CHAPTER 18

We met at the criminal courthouse where Sam was to be arraigned. I felt sick, and my body shook from the nervousness. I wished I could turn back the clock. Instead, I had to face this with Sam's mother. She had found the attorney earlier that morning and hired him to take the case on the spot. We both knew Sam's future was at stake and prayed he was good at his job.

The lawyer informed us that it was too early in the case to make any assumptions. He mentioned many legal facts in conversation. I was lost for the most part but I vaguely remember he said something about how there had been federal laws enacted which stipulated a mandatory minimum penalty for certain drug offenses. He added that Sam's case was a state case and that was to his advantage. He repeated that he needed time to go over the facts and reminded us that the only objective that morning was to get him out on bail.

Much later I learned of the "drug-free zone law" which imposed increased penalties for drug offenses committed near schools. I felt so stupid! This all could have gone much worse if it would have happened the night of my prom in the school parking lot. It was an indication of Sam's immature, ignorant, and reckless behavior. I realized we were so young and thoughtless, and never fully understood the gravity of our actions, not to mention the fact that we had no concept of the legal consequences to our poor choices. Ready or not, we were about to take a very unpleasant crash course.

I was anxious about the seriousness of the charges. I imagined there would be a heavy punishment for dealing cocaine. I was confused because Sam lived in New York and he committed the crime in the state of New Jersey. The attorney explained that New Jersey state authorities had jurisdiction because they were the entity that apprehended him. His residency in New York did not make this a federal case, it only meant that if he were released on bail then he'd have the burden of traveling to New Jersey for all future legal proceedings. The attorney reiterated that Sam's case was a state case and this was favorable from a legal standpoint since there was a possibility of harsher consequences as determined by certain federal statutes. He relieved our panic by further informing us that the court considered mitigating factors before determining whether or not to grant bail. In this case, a mitigating factor could be the fact that this was Sam's first offense. Also, in this particular incident, it appeared that the exchange involved a relatively small amount of the illegal substance. He went on to state that these were favorable factors and the court might consider them when determining whether or not to exercise some leniency. My only hope in that moment was that he would get the court's mercy and be granted bail.

At the arraignment we learned some of the specifics of the case. It turned out the drug sting was a set up. My suspicions had been confirmed. The young man Sam was dealing with was acting as an informant for the New Jersey Attorney General's office. This person had been caught dealing and, rather than facing a hefty drug conviction, had opted to plea-bargain with the prosecution. It was uncertain if he was offered a very low sentence or exoneration in exchange for assisting the prosecution with the conviction of other persons. My mouth dropped. I knew it! I felt it! Why did Sam ignore my instincts? Now it was too late! Sam would have to deal with this mess and I would have to stick around to see him through it. Forget all the plans to go away to college! Forget getting away from it all! I felt this nightmare would never end. Overwhelmed by my assumption of what was to come, I let out a burst of tears. It was so hard to control my emotions, I could barely catch my breath. I felt I was too young to be involved in this mess. and felt sorry for myself. Sam's mother held me as if she understood why I was crying.

The attorney noticed how young and distraught I was and, in an effort to simmer the intensity he repeated, "The State of New Jersey has jurisdiction over Sam's case. This is a good factor. Federal cases allow a judge to place additional penalties, so hang in there. It's his first offense. Just hang in there."

At the arraignment, commonly known as bail hearing, the court bailiff called out his case, "Docket number ---- The People of the State of New Jersey against Sam..." I felt like I was going to vomit. I couldn't even look at Sam as he was taken out of the holding pen and into the courtroom. He was placed to stand to the right of his attorney in front of the judge, wearing an orange jumpsuit. He was shackled, defeated, quiet, vulnerable. It broke my heart.

I saw the prosecution facing the judge and ready to hit us with justice. There was some scurrying of paperwork as Sam just stood still. Sam's attorney stated he would waive the reading of charges in the interest of moving on with the proceedings. He continued, "It is the defendant's first offense, Your Honor. He lives with his mother and sister and poses absolutely no threat of fleeing. I request the court release him on his own recognizance."

The prosecutor argued, "The defendant is not a resident of the state of New Jersey and has no attachment to the community. He has serious charges against him and therefore, we emphasize he does post a risk of fleeing. Your Honor, we respectfully request he is held on a one hundred thousand dollar bail." My heart sank! $100,000.00? We can't afford that! I was anxious for his release, and was afraid Sam was not strong enough to stop a bully from beating him up. Worse yet, I didn't think he could defend himself against a predator who might want to do unspeakable things to him. The court denied the defense attorney's request and Sam's bail was set at $100,000.00. For a split second I had to catch my breath. My legs felt weak. I sat quietly and heard the judge as he specified it was set payable in a bond requiring a ten percent cash payment. I immediately breathed a sigh of relief. I looked at his mother and said, "$10,000.00? Is that what the Judge meant? That's an attainable figure, right?"

She looked at me and said, "Yes, I'll get the details from the attorney on what to do next."

Bail was set and the court bailiff escorted Sam back to the prisoners' holding area of the courtroom. Sam was to remain in jail until his mother could post bail.

We left the courtroom as the attorney explained, "If you are arrested on a felony charge and the arrest happens in a state other than your home state, then it is unlikely that any judge will release you on your own recognizance. The assumption is that the defendant does not have strong ties to the community in the state he is arrested in and, thereby, is a higher risk of fleeing. Therefore, in almost every case, the defendant is likely to be required to post bail. Bail is a guarantee to the court that you will come back for further proceedings. It does not mean he is guilty, so please don't be alarmed. Also, I know a licensed bail bondsman that can help you. He's probably going to want some kind of collateral from you, but don't worry, there is no risk. Only if a defendant fails to appear in court are bail monies kept and properties seized. I am confident that will not be the case for you guys. So here is his business card, call him as soon as you leave here. The case was adjourned pending action by a Grand Jury, at which time it will be determined if Sam will be indicted."

The attorney spoke confidently and it helped us trust him. He was able to find out that the informant in the case would be the witness against Sam. Fortunately, Sam did not resist nor did he make any incriminating statements to the police at the time of his arrest. I thought, "Thank goodness, he was probably too scared to talk. I bet he thought he was doomed with a solid case against him and was shocked."

His mother and I left the courtroom and returned to her house. She called the licensed bail bondsman who requested information on her home. Fortunately, Sam's mother did not have a mortgage on her house. She owned it outright and would be able to use it as collateral. She could secure the bond for bail by using her house, and my father offered to give her the $10,000.00 required in cash. She refused to accept the money from him. I assured her it came from my mother who felt the same way she did. I convinced her to accept my parents' money and she was then able to attain the bond for Sam's bail.

Sam's mother was chain smoking as she shared feeling nervous about the long-term possibilities. She was a loving mother who wanted her son's release from jail. She had no doubt that her son would face the court and answer for the charges against him. She was certain Sam would never run from the law and there would be no risk of her losing her house. Nevertheless, we were informed that Sam would probably have to appear in court multiple times after his release. Since she was determined to accompany him every step of the way, she knew this would take a toll on her work schedule. She worried she'd have to miss many days of work to deal with all the court obligations pending Sam's trial, and prayed she would not lose her job. The fact that the case was in New Jersey and they lived in Staten Island, New York made the whole thing even more burdensome. For now, we were relieved that he could deal with this problem in the comfort of his home instead of in a jail cell.

Unbeknown to me, the real nightmare for me began after Sam was released on bail. Some time had gone by since his arrest and I was now a full-time college student and a full-time worker. Sam became very demanding of my company. If I couldn't visit him or I was too busy to cater to his needs, he would stage asthma episodes and countless other crisis situations. I felt forced to spend time with him even when I was not up to it. All the consideration I had felt toward him was disappearing. Once again, he had become an incredible stress factor in my life. I hung in there and continued to be as patient as I could with him.

Sam's indictment was a certainty, mainly because there was a witness working with the prosecution's office willing to testify against him. I didn't know much about the legal system but was interested in finding out as much as I could. I was motivated in part because I wanted to determine how long my "sentence" would be. I felt my life depended on the case's outcome and yearned for some control over the matter. I feared the possibility that Sam, like his former friend, negotiated with the prosecution in order to reduce his sentence. Contemplating this thought kept me up at night. I was fearful that my father was at great risk. It was these fears that turned me into Sam's slave. He was very needy and I felt obligated to answer his every beck and call. I grew extremely resentful of Sam and wished I didn't have to deal with him at all. I would later learn things that would indicate the prosecution did try to bargain with Sam, but at the time it was frustrating to know this problem would probably not go away for a long time to come.

Sam's mother and Sam excluded me from the meetings with Sam's attorney. I was desperate to keep informed. I read as much as possible about the legal proceedings in similar cases and found several helpful resources. There was a bulletin released by The U.S. Department of Justice, which revealed information about felony sentences in state courts during the year 1986. It indicated several statistical facts. In relation to drug cases, only 37% of the convicted drug traffickers were sentenced to prison, 27% to local jails, and 35%

go straight to probation. I know Sam needed to pay society retribution, but as terrible as it sounds, I prayed Sam would fall under the 35% percent. I prayed on my knees for the miracle of probation. I wanted out of the situation and felt absolutely obligated to see him through it. I was, for all intents and purposes, trapped until the case was resolved. I used the information I'd learn to cheer Sam up. He needed frequent pep talks and more encouragement than I could give. I would ask him to hang steady, while all along I secretly hoped he would not implicate anyone else.

I encouraged Sam to see the bright side of his situation. I remembered what his attorney had said and continuously reminded him that dealing with the courts in the state of New Jersey was much easier than the federal court system. I tried to raise his spirits so I explained my reasoning by referring back to an article I had read regarding the federal government having initiated the 1986 Act. I explained it was basically a federal criminal law, which made distinctions between "cocaine base", and other forms of cocaine, for example, crack. Sam became furious when I mentioned this to him. "Josefina! I'm not completely unethical! As terrible as dealing cocaine was, crack is a despicable drug! I never would have messed with that!"

He was telling the truth and I had to sincerely apologize. "Sam, I'm sorry! I'm trying to help you. I didn't compare you to a low life criminal. I know you're not like that. It's irrelevant to you. I believe you just made a mistake, that's all." I barely had anymore left in me, but I continued and prayed for strength.

I continued to read as much as I could about the law and similar cases but was very careful not to mention anything else to Sam. I suppose I was not very good at doing research. Most of the information I learned was about the federal government and irrelevant to Sam's case, but it still served as a comfort to me.

Reading about how the system works relieved my anxiety since Sam and his mother kept me in the dark. I also learned a system to rank offenders had been created. Penalties imposed on offenders were determined by how they ranked in relation to their crime. There were references using terms like "major drug dealer." This essentially referred to the manufacturers or the heads of organizations who are responsible for creating and delivering very large quantities; "H.R. Rep. No. 845, 99th Cong., 2d Sess. pt. 1, at 16-17 (1986)." This type of offense required a minimum sentence of ten years. There was also the term "serious trafficker." A serious trafficker is considered a manager of the retail level traffic, the person who is filling the bags, packaging, etc. and doing so in substantial street quantities. That offense required a minimum sentence of five years. In Sam's case, I wondered... What sentence did the law require for a complete idiot?

I used the information for comfort, but in the end I really had no idea what lay ahead. I only focused on the fact that he had been caught with a relatively small amount, did not have any prior offenses, and was not part of a gang or anything of the sort. I made the deduction that he probably ranked as a minor offender and continued to pray for a quick resolve.

CHAPTER 19

Sam was indicted at a county courthouse. He pled guilty to lesser charges, which I was ignorant to because I continued to be kept in the dark by Sam and his mother. I remember multiple court appearances. I think his attorney proceeded to negotiate or buy time in an effort to get Sam the lowest possible sentence. I didn't feel I had a right to liberate myself until his legal problems were completely resolved, but I kept busy and tried to be in his presence the least amount of time possible.

Although I was not included in the meetings with Sam's attorney, I didn't demand much because I still feared he could implicate my father in his dealings. I had once cared about Sam and sincerely wished all his legal troubles were over; however, at this point, the main reasons I stayed connected to Sam were my wanting to protect my father, and feeling sorry for him. I reluctantly continued to carry on with Sam while I hated everything about our relationship. Every moment was torturous, especially the few times I felt obligated to have sex with him. He thought I had a problem and was frigid. He refused to see that I didn't want it with him. Sex with Sam now felt unnatural, unsatisfying, fake and shameful. I wanted to avoid the intimacy. I knew a sure and quick way to satisfy him was through oral sex so I opted to offer it, although I hated it. I wanted to scream to his face that I hated sex with him! The heavy burdens from my past mistakes were becoming increasingly difficult to bear. The relationship continued to dangle by a doomed thread as I symbolically carried a cross, not just because of guilt but also to protect my father and because I believed I had to pay back some retribution for my part in the mistakes we made. I made up my mind and promised myself to endure it until Sam's debt to society was paid.

For a while we had put the incident aside and had moved forward with life in general. While waiting for the court to impose a sentence, Sam switched out of the electrician school where he had found trouble. He finished his education at another facility and received an electrician certification. He went on to work at his father electrical company. I, outside of my work and school duties, was living in a state of perpetual unhappiness. I felt intolerant to Sam but had also become conditioned to continuing with him. Sam became a disciplined employee for his father and I continued as a full time worker and college student. We did not have much in common except we both felt sorry that we were ever involved with drugs. I was sorry not just because it was illegal, but also because I realized it was morally reprehensible. I think Sam was sorry because he was caught and he had realized there truly are no shortcuts to success.

We were working hard to get our lives back on track while awaiting the outcome of his case. Unfortunately, like a debt, our efforts were only paying the accumulated interest; for all our positive changes we still owed the principal. Sam's pending jail sentence, like a black cloud, hovered over us for three years, at which time Sam's attorney negotiated terms that were acceptable to him. The time to pay back the entire debt had finally arrived.

The lawyer had explained that the prison system considered certain factors to reduce time spent in prison. He explained there were various options. For instance, the "good-time credits" were based on good institutional behavior, which offered several days per month to be reduced off the sentence. He advised that if Sam consistently received such credit, it could add up to a significant 60 days off per year. Meaning, in a calendar year he might end up serving ten months instead of the twelve. It was all very confusing to me but still good news.

When the whole fiasco began, I read as a form of consolation. I read everything I could find about our prison system. I learned its purpose was to obtain retribution, to incapacitate an offender from committing additional crimes, to deter people from getting involved in criminal activities, and to rehabilitate society's offenders. I read horror stories about how petty offenders made connections in prison with hard-core criminals that ultimately resulted in their transformation into serious delinquents. This made me wonder if the system could have the opposite effect and put Sam's progress at risk? There was no way to know for certain. I had finally reached the point where I had to stop and distance myself from the subject matter, as it had become more torturous than helpful. I decided to give up trying to understand any of it and to simply have faith that all was in God's hands. This decision was very comforting for me. I clearly saw that none of it was within my reach to fix. I understood that trusting in a higher power was the only way I could get through this problem.

As for Sam, I knew he was struggling to understand the importance of having to serve any time. He felt he had worked hard to get his life straightened out and believed he had been rehabilitated since he had no interest in participating in any other criminal activity. He did not want to be part of anything that would jeopardize his future and felt he didn't need prison to help him understand the already-learned lesson. Serving time for the sole purpose of retribution seemed unfair since he considered the agony of uncertainty during the past three years of his life to be enough punishment. I hoped his fears would not weaken the progress he had made, but I couldn't help but agree that after three long years, an incarceration was a conflicting and difficult concept to understand. I, too, did not see the point or purpose to incarcerating Sam. He did not need to be incapacitated since he had been deterred from all criminal activities and was well on his way to complete rehabilitation. I felt his retribution could involve community service instead of a jail sentence. It was all frustrating and difficult for us to process. I remained concerned he might become the target of a bully. He did not look intimidating and his dependency on me proved him to be weak. I did not think he'd have the courage to stick up for himself. On the flip side, I also contemplated the slim possibility he could make connections with the wrong element. It would be a tragedy if a prison sentence were his reentry ticket to additional criminal activity. I believed he had changed, repented, and rehabilitated. I hoped that when he entered the prison system he would not regress, making it all pointless. I shared this concern with Sam. He, in turn, shared that he still had big dreams and the difference now was that he wanted to earn his success; however, I understood if Sam decided to regress it would no longer be my problem.

In the deepest, most private part of my thoughts laid my greatest contradiction; although I did not want Sam in prison, I was anxious to start a new life away from him. There were times when I had viewed his potential prison time to be a saving grace, an opportunity to finally get the separation I desperately needed.

Sam had agreed to a guilty plea so, despite the efforts he had made to recover or the beliefs he had about the fairness of it all, there was one inevitable fact; he had to serve time. Sam's attorney negotiated a five-year "flat" or determinate sentence. This meant the court had the authority to set a fixed period of incarceration; he did not have a minimum or maximum term. It was arranged that he would serve six months in a state prison, then go on to live in a half-way house after his release. After he served a couple of months in the half-way house, he would begin a period of house arrest. During his house arrest he would be monitored through the use of an electronic system. This provided him the opportunity, as a convicted felon, to slowly reenter society. Sam was to wear an ankle bracelet to ensure he would live up to the agreement to only leave the house for work purposes. The ankle bracelet monitored his location at all times. He had to adhere to the restricted traveling privileges and a set curfew. Traveling to predetermined locations was allowed during the specified work scheduled hours. He was to live in the half-way house for two years and then enter a period of post-release supervision. This meant he could resume his normal activities so long as he reported to a probation officer. This arrangement was to start in mid-December. I felt relieved and could not wait to start the countdown. Six months seemed like a fair exchange. I had imagined a worse outcome for Sam. Still, part of me felt sorry for him. I was absolutely certain that after I served my duty I would close this chapter of my life for good.

The day Sam turned himself in I said a prayer and asked that God forgive me. I couldn't wait to get away from him. I could finally get a break from his unwanted affection and start planning my future. Ironically, his incarceration made me feel free for the first time in five years. I was fifteen years old when I met him and since that time, he possessed me like his personal property and I was ready to break loose. Prison robbed him of the ability to monitor my every move. It was liberating, exhilarating, joyous! I still felt obligated to visit him on Sunday and receive his daily phone call, but that was a tolerable arrangement.

While Sam served his short prison term, I was able to make new friends for the first time since I had lost touch with Dana. I made social plans with people other than Sam. It was an opportunity to lift the heavy load and walk without a daily dosage of fear. I was busy as a full time employee and student at the community college. It was exhausting and awesome at the same time. After five years I finally had ownership of my life. I was a twenty-year-old girl who wanted to execute a simple plan; stay with Sam until all his legal troubles were over, and then disconnect completely from him. I admitted I had played a part in his failures but truly felt I had assumed responsibility and paid a high price.

Soon after Sam was incarcerated, Sam's mother asked me to pick up legal documents relating to his case at his attorney's office. She was exhausted and did not feel up to traveling to New Jersey. The manila envelope was not sealed. I was a curious girl so I decided to take a peek. To my shock, Sam had divulged Father's name and made incriminating statements about him in an effort to avoid serving his jail sentence. I was angry and in complete disbelief. I don't know if I would have behaved differently if I had been aware of his betrayal, but I wished I had been given a choice. I was fuming when he phoned that evening. I confronted him, "You're an immature coward! You couldn't deal with the consequences of your actions! You're a liar and a traitor." I was so angry I did not want to hear his voice. I did not give him a chance to respond, and I hung up the phone and ran in my bedroom. I didn't know what to do about it. I pondered whether or not I should say anything to anyone. I thought too much time had gone by and assumed it indicated Sam's testimony bared no consequences on my father.

CHAPTER 20

Soon after Sam turned himself in, on a day like every other, I arrived home from work when the doorbell rang. Gabriel answered the door. A man was standing at the front door. He asked, "Are you Octavio Lopez?"

My brother stated, "No."

The man looked through the opening of the door. He tried to get as good a look as possible and take in as much information as he could through the small opening. "Is Octavio Lopez home?"

"No."

"Do you know when he'll be home?"

"No idea."

"Do you know Octavio Lopez?"

"Yes, that's my dad but he's not home."

The man, unsatisfied with the information he gathered so far asked, "Do you have a picture of him I can see?"

"No, I don't. Why?"

"At what time do you expect him home? Can we come in?"

"I'm not sure. No, you can't come in. I'm not sure how long he'll be."

"Why can't we come in? What's the big deal?"

"Because I don't know you. You're a stranger and you can't come in my house. I'm calling the cops!"

"It's not necessary to call the cops. I am a federal agent. I work for the Federal Bureau of Investigations."

Gabriel gave the man a blank stare, a clear indication he felt confused. The man went on, "I'm with the federal government and I have a subpoena for Octavio Lopez. It's ok, kid. I'll just come back later."

Appearing baffled, Gabriel closed the door and said to me, "Josefina! That's really weird, he wanted to see a picture of Dad."

I had been standing nearby and heard most of the conversation. I felt the butterflies in my stomach tingle. "Really? That is strange. Who is he?"

"He said he's a federal agent and he has a subpoena for Dad."

"Subpoena, for Dad? Why?"

"I don't know." As Gabriel walked toward the door, I looked out the window.

"Oh my god, Gabriel! A man just walked to the front from our back yard and there's another guy on the side of the house."

We stood silent, looking out the window. Gabriel said, "Look, they both just walked across the street." We watched as they each got into separate cars. "Oh look Josefina! There are other guys with them. Josefina, what is this? It's freaking me out!

"I don't know. Me too. I don't know. Let's call Mom!"

My brother looked out the window as I walked toward the kitchen to grab the phone. I was about to dial Mother when he called out, "Josefina!" He noticed Father was parking his car in front of the house.

He called out to me again, "Josefina, Dad is home!"

I said to my brother, "Good, let's go outside and tell him about the men parked across the street."

Gabriel opened the front door. I was about to go outside when I saw Father step out of the car holding a couple of bags filled with groceries. Gabriel and I walked outside and down the steps in front of the house toward him when all of a sudden, as if in a movie, we saw a few men coming out of the two unmarked cars parked across from our house. In my mind, everything slowed down. I could see as they left the car doors open and rushed toward Father. Gabriel and I watched in absolute disbelief. They were repeatedly yelling, "Freeze, put your hands up high where we can see them!" Father showed no resistance. He quietly put the grocery bags on the sidewalk and put his hands up. Gabriel and I loved Father, and hated this moment.

Gabriel began to cry uncontrollably as he ran up to the man that had knocked on the door moments earlier and said, "You tricked me! You told me you only needed to speak to him! What are you doing?"

The officer responded, "Kid, go back in the house! We are taking him to the local police station. We need you to step away. We have a warrant for his arrest. Kid! I'm serious! Walk back into your house! Your father is under arrest."

I was speechless. There was nothing we could do. I saw Gabriel trying to hold Father. The agent ordered him to stop but he could not control himself. He walked again toward Father in an effort to hold him. Father nodded his head at Gabriel indicating that he back off and go in the house. Gabriel finally listened and backed away. One of the other men in the group took Father's wallet, removed his driver's license and returned the wallet along with the car keys to me. I looked at Father as he was being handcuffed. I felt devastated. I wanted to protect him but there was nothing Gabriel or I could do.

"Gabriel! Let's go back in the house. We need to call Mother at work." Unfortunately there was no answer at her office. I was so stressed out, my body was shaking. This feeling was familiar. I couldn't believe I'd have to go through it again. The anxiety became so overwhelming that I felt a need to hold on tight to Gabriel. We cried and hugged each other until I felt uncomfortably hot. I was covered in sweat and felt the urge to use the bathroom. I was afraid my dad would be put in a prison for a long time. I knew the legal system was scary and what lay ahead for Father would not be easy on our family. I went back to the kitchen phone and tried calling Mother again. There was still no answer so we waited outside about twenty minutes before Mother arrived from work.

Mother knew immediately something was wrong. She looked at me and asked, "What happened?" I told her that Father had been arrested. She stood very still and did not show much emotion. Mother was never one to react to serious situations, she always stayed in control. This time I wanted her to show emotion, as if it were an indication that she still loved him and wanted to help him, but she kept surprisingly calm and asked me to calm down. She hurried into the house, picked up the phone, and called Mami Abuela's sister, her aunt, Tia Elvi.

Tia Elvi was an attractive, strong woman who had demonstrated she had the ability to deal with difficult situations. She had been the first person to initially migrate to the United States from Colombia. I had always admired her daring sense of adventure. She had moved to a new country alone and without a support system. She never asked for anyone's assistance and earned everything through hard work. She had a progressive mentality for a woman of her times. Tia Elvi's ideas about women in general were admirable. She was proud to be self-sufficient and independent. She always criticized Mami Abuela's childbearing habits, believing it impoverished and robbed Mami Abuela's ability to make way for a better life. Tia Elvi had helped Mami Abuela's children attain visas and eventually legal residence in America. The aunts and uncles admired her. Naturally, I was not surprised Mother looked to her for help in our desperate hour of need.

Tia Elvi immediately drove to our house. Mother gave her the little information we had. She reacted as we expected she would. She knew a good lawyer she could call in the morning, and agreed to accompany us to the local police station.

We arrived at the police station and spoke to a uniformed officer at the front desk. He informed us that Father had only been kept there for a short while and had already been transported to the county prison. Tia Elvi asked the officer, "Well! How are we to know where the county jail is? We need the address! Where have they taken him?"

I can recall feeling sick and partially embarrassed. I was glad Tia Elvi was there to represent us. Our family knew some of the police officers in the area from participating in several community events, like the town musical concerts, art fairs, Easter egg hunts, the spring Bar-b-que, the Christmas parades, and so on. Obviously, they recognized who we were and it felt shameful. We left and drove to the county jail where we were told we would not be able to see him until the next day. Mother destabilized for a short moment. She hugged Tia Elvi as if she was a child and asked if we could spend the night at her house. "Yes, of course. I was taking you home with me anyway. Tomorrow is another day. We'll see him tomorrow. For tonight, let's just get some rest because we are going to need it."

That night Tia Elvi was our saving grace. She gladly agreed to accommodate us at her home providing Mother, Gabriel, and me with much needed comfort. I could hear Mother whisper to Tia Elvi, "We are so lucky the authorities did not have a warrant for our car or house." I felt tired of it all. I wanted to be away from the entire situation but once again, I had no choice.

The next morning I was the first one to wake up. It was 6:30 a.m. but I was wide-awake so I decided to shower. By the time I came out of the shower, Mother and Tia Elvi were speaking about what we needed to do to help Father. Tia Elvi assured us her friend was a very good attorney. She said, "If he can't help us, don't worry, he'll refer us to someone he trusts." This was a good start for Mother since she didn't know how she could find a good criminal attorney. I broke down and let Mother know what I had read in some of the documents related to Sam's arrest. She was not angry, she gave me a compassionate look and said, "Don't stress Josefina. Let's first find out what the charges are before we make any assumptions." I was glad to no longer carry this secret. It had consumed me and I felt relieved that it was now out in the open.

As promised, by 9:00 a.m. Tia Elvi called her friend who scheduled a meeting with us for 11:00 a.m. that day. The attorney made several calls, gathering some details, then informed us that Father had a warrant for his arrest related to a federal case that was pending against him which dated back a couple of years. Evidently, the FBI had put out a search for Father in Dade County, Miami, Florida a few years earlier. His name and address were apparently floating in the system and had recently resurfaced on their computer database. We could only speculate it might have been related to Sam's allegations but never found any proof that could confirm the assumption.

In my understanding of things, Father was not a fugitive since he was not deliberately running from the law. He was unaware that he had been implicated in an old drug case. He kept his driver's license with his current home address, the utilities as well as all his affairs were handled under his birth name without any attempt to hide his identity, he had no aliases or disguises, and our bank mortgage was under his and Mother's names. How Father had all of a sudden been sought after was a real mystery. It all kept leading back to the possibility that Sam had unknowingly sounded off an alarm, but there was no evidence that Father's arrest was in any way related to Sam's claims. To my absolute relief, at a much later time I would learn that the authorities could not find sufficient evidence to verify a connection between Father and Sam. It had been decided that no further investigation would be conducted in the matter relating to them.

As the facts of the case came to light, we would find out that Father had been indirectly involved in a transaction between friends of his working out of Miami, Florida and undercover FBI agents. Ironically, Father gained no financial benefit in that particular deal. He, as a favor to a friend, served as an English translator during the negotiations. At the New Jersey Criminal Court House, an FBI Agent took the witness stand and testified he recognized Father as one of the persons in the group involved in the drug deal. He verified that Father was specifically introduced as a translator. It was difficult for me to start this new nightmare having just been through Sam's ordeal, but the fact that in this particular instance Father was not dealing personal merchandise or accepting money for his own gain was a lucky break. He was inconsequential in this particular deal in relation to the other Colombian dealers, but his involvement was enough to get a judge to extradite him to Miami, Florida where he would have to face the charges against him.

In a desperate attempt to help Father after he was extradited to Miami, Mother looked into Santeria, which is a syncretic religion influenced by Roman Catholicism and made popular in Cuba, Dominican Republic, Haiti, Colombia, and many other places. Mother knew the power cult priests had to influence the spirit world, and respected the possibility that this could be a way to help Father. She heard of a Santera from the Dominican Republic who lived in The Bronx. The female priest was of African descent and was known to possess extraordinary powers sure to help difficult cases.

Mother visited the Santera who performed a Caracoles reading, also known as the Merindilogun consultation. Caracoles are cowrie shells with the backs removed and specially consecrated. She read Mother's fortune and, more importantly, Father's problem. After completing the divination she assured Mother she could help Father's problem and put their lives back in harmony. She stated that her saints demanded reverence in order to reduce the legal consequences to little or no time in jail. She instructed Mother to do a cleansing and sponsor a ceremonial ritual as an offering to demonstrate worship to the saints who would intercede on this major issue. The ceremony would include a feast with foods that appealed to her saints, cigars, and a live chicken, which would be sacrificed as part of the ritual.

Mother sent Gabriel and me over to the woman's apartment with money to cover the expenses necessary to honor the saints. The

Santera opened the door dressed in a white outfit. She had a big voice and a loud laugh that projected as if she had a microphone attached to her vocal chords. Her dark skin accentuated the white of her teeth as she welcomed us into her home. I wasn't sure why but I felt an inexplicable nervousness as Gabriel and I walked into this very peculiar place. We were surprised to see the beautiful feast displayed near her shrine. There were statues everywhere in a corner of her living room, what looked like a fire pit, and in another corner near the main wall she displayed an elaborate altar with beautiful royal blue, white, and red satins draped over a shrine. The shrine was ornately adorning where a statue of a goddess, possibly the Virgen de la Caridad del Cobre or Santa Barbara, stood surrounded by an array of fresh fruits, candies, and flowers. There were also a few dishes of cooked food on cracked and chipped plates and a live chicken ready for the Santera to sacrifice. The animal's blood was to be used as an act of communion with the spirits. She explained that the offerings near the shrine represented a prayer to give thanks and worship the saints.

The Santera looked at Gabriel and said, "You're a nonbeliever." Gabriel was only eighteen years old at the time and had no idea what she was talking about. He responded by laughing. She asked him to have a seat so she could look over his spirit and offered him an opportunity to secretly ask the saint three questions. Other than Father's problem, Gabriel really didn't have any personal concerns, so he secretly asked if Father would be fine. The Santera flipped the caracoles and said, "One does not ask questions one knows the answer to." She asked him to think of his next question. He wanted to trick her so he secretly asked the same question. She shook the caracoles in her hand, flipped them onto the table where they landed on the same exact combination. She looked at him with an angry face and said, "Young man, you've wasted a question." He was shocked she knew he was trying to trick her and apologized, so she still granted him his last question. Gabriel thought about it but couldn't figure out what else he was curious about, so he thought about his history mid-term exam. In his mind he asked if he would pass the test. She rolled the caracoles and responded, "Yes, just take a clear glass, fill it with water and place it near you in that moment."

She proceeded to light up a cigar while I looked around and noticed several coconuts, a walking stick, and a chicken violently flapping its wings in a small crate near a corner of the room. She spoke in a foreign language and performed rhythmic moves while chanting to invoke the spirits who would intercede and aid Father at the time he was to face the judge in Miami. In a million years I would have never believed what happened next had it not been because I was there. The Santera, apparently in a trance or possessed by the spirits, grabbed the walking stick and slammed it with brutal force on the floor, creating a deafening sound. My heart nearly stopped when I looked at the walking stick as it transformed before my very eyes into a living, slithering snake. I felt a chill go up my spine. This was no magic trick! I was terrified and fascinated at the same time. She proceeded to transform the animal back into a stick and walked past the center of the room where she had placed a large wooden bowl. She bent down near the corner where the small crate lay, continuing her chanting while she went on to the divination phase of the ceremony. She proceeded to open the front door of the small crate and grabbed the panicked bird. With a strong grip, she held its body and pulled it out of the small box. Later the Santera explained that the chicken was killed mercifully and that it felt no pain. Still, I felt sorry for the animal. It was difficult to watch as she twisted the neck slightly to one side and proceeded to sever the carotid artery with a knife. Blood gushed out as she aimed the chicken downward and poured the blood into the wooden bowl. The animal was sacrificed so Father could get the mercy of the court. Gabriel and I held hands and struggled to remain calm.

Gabriel's eyes were ready to pop out of his face, and his jaw dropped significantly. I noticed my mouth was wide open and I regained control of my emotions to appear to be cool with the ritual. For a moment I thought my brother looked like a zombie. I could barely look at him and was afraid I might burst out laughing. I always had a nervous laugh problem, causing people to question why I laughed during a serious situation. It is not something I can control and I've often found myself forced to explain it. I battled against my natural instinct, as I did not want the Santera to misunderstand. I bit my lip and tightened all my facial expressions. If I had a mirror I might have seen what Gabriel noticed at that moment.

We left her house feeling very confident that Father would be fine, as well as slightly amused. Gabriel told me I looked like an idiot or someone who had accidentally been hit in the head with a frying pan. I responded that he looked like someone who was hit with the dumb stick. We laughed as he swore he was going to follow the Santera's advice about his history exam.

Our confidence was reinforced by what happened to Gabriel in school the day of his history exam. He followed the Santera's instructions, and walked into class with a clear glass of water. He was surprised to see that no one paid attention to how unusual this was. He proceeded to place the glass on the windowsill nearest to him. The test began and he was so confident that he would pass without a glitch that he never bothered to study. While everyone was quietly working on the test, he proceeded to open up his textbook. He openly placed the textbook on his lap, read, and wrote the answer on his test paper. The teacher walked around the classroom as she always did during test time, and passed by Gabriel several times without making mention of his blatant cheating. That afternoon Gabriel was very excited when he got home from school. He said, "Josefina, we need not worry about a thing! Father will be home soon enough."

"Why do you say that?"

"So, today at school…" He was amazed at the fact that the teacher did not see his obvious cheating. I am still not convinced that his cheating was that obvious but the incident made Gabriel a believer. He accepted as proof that whatever the Santera had done for Father would be one hundred percent effective.

Mother, Gabriel, and I traveled to Miami. Luckily, Father's niece lived in Florida, and Mother arranged for my cousin to pick us up at the airport. She was one of Father's brothers' daughters. She let us stay at her house and had helped us find a great defense attorney. The attorney was known as one of the top criminal defense attorneys in the state of Florida. He openly shared he knew the prosecutor and the judge assigned to Father's case. He was confident Father's case would have a favorable outcome, and I recall feeling relieved after our meeting with him.

Father went before a magistrate for a bail hearing. The proceedings were relatively painless. Despite the fact that the judge knew Father lived in New Jersey and would be travelling back to his home state after bail was granted, he did not hesitate to grant terms similar to Sam's; 10 percent cash on a $150,000.00 bond. The attorney explained that Father had no prior legal record and was not a risk of flight since his wife, children, job, and property were all well established in the United States. We left the courtroom and Mother drove the rental car to a bondsman. We all knew the drill, so she had the necessary paperwork to place our home as collateral to secure the bond. Our attorney completed all the necessary paperwork and before the day was over, Father was released from jail. We spent an additional day in Florida enjoying the beautiful weather before we returned home to New Jersey, accompanied by Father.

While Father's case underwent the normal legal proceedings, he visited several doctors and ended up spending a week in the hospital due to a bleeding ulcer. His stress had gotten the best of his nervous system. He hoped his medical condition would be a mitigating factor for the court to consider before rendering a decision in his case. He requested his doctors provide medical letters addressed to the court that explained his ill health. He also asked that people in his life write character letters addressed to the judge that would paint a picture of the real person. He wanted the judge to know he was a regular guy, a father, husband, neighbor, parishioner, and a friend to many. It was interesting to see that, in fact, he was all those things; not entirely bad but not entirely good.

Sam had served his time in prison, as well as his time in the half-way house, and was now at the house arrest phase of his sentence. He was under strict monitoring and was allowed to leave the house during work hours only. He was obligated to return to his restricted environment and received a confirmation phone call every day to ensure he was obeying the agreement. He and I could not wait to end the period of house arrest. He was anxious to regain all his freedoms. He accepted the occasional reporting to a probation officer until the five year flat sentence was completed as a lesser affliction. I can't explain why, but although I highly resented his betrayal, I continued to lend him emotional support. It was excruciating but I accepted his phone calls and kept visiting him. I punished myself and believed it was my moral obligation to keep to my original plan of seeing him through all his legal troubles. I justified it by convincing myself that he was not directly responsible for my father's troubles and, therefore, still deserved my consideration.

During one of my visits while he was under house arrest, we were watching a movie in his living room, and Sam began to kiss me and touch me. Although I was not interested in sexual relations with him, he was very persistent and would not quit touching me and pestering me. It had been a long while since we had sex and I didn't want to encourage him by getting myself on birth control. I tried to divert his attention but all my efforts to put him off were in vain. I reluctantly accepted his advances and let him take my underwear off. I warned him that I was not on any form of birth control and that he should be careful. He ignored me.

I know it's hard to understand, but even though it was consensual, the whole thing felt ugly and dirty, and all I thought about was that it would be over soon. Thankfully it was quick! As soon as it was over I felt panic all over my body. I immediately got dressed and left his house completely distraught. I couldn't believe I had allowed this to happen. It was infuriating.

Sam phoned me that night, but I did not want to speak to him. The thought of a possible lifetime attachment to him was absolutely absurd. It contradicted my plan to be free of Sam after he was done with his house arrest. A part of me believed he had premeditated this encounter as a way to force me to stay with him. He must have known I was with him out of duty, not love. Nothing made sense in that moment. I couldn't understand why he would still want to be with me. He was unable to see that our relationship had passed its charm long ago. Now, the only feelings that remained for me were regrets.

Mother had never really talked about sex with me. I assumed that she thought I was a virgin since I prided myself on having strong Catholic convictions, and she treated me like a young child when it came to sex. Mother meant well but she was ignorant about the reality of teenage behavior. She came from a culture where young ladies were guarded by chaperones, and precautionary measures were taken to ensure there was no privacy between young couples until the time of marriage. Mother grew up in a strict environment that only fell short of placing "chastity belts" to protect a woman's virginity. She would never engage in premarital sex and expected I would follow the same protocol. Her lack of communication with me proved to be a dangerous thing. I could not confide in her when I was a teenager with a head filled with fantasies about the things I believed and wanted. As time passed, I realized my emotions and thoughts about things and people had changed. My feelings for Sam were gone and he had a difficult time accepting it. I had unwillingly allowed him to engage intimately with me. I should have adamantly refused. I had blamed many of my poor decisions on my youth and inexperience, but this time I admit I knew the relationship was dead so I should have exercised the power of abstinence or, at minimum, the power of protecting my own body. Sam refused to understand why I was so upset. He thought if I was expecting that everything would turn out fine; we would simply speak to my parents and marry sooner rather than later. I tried not to panic, but it was difficult for me to sleep, eat, or do anything productive. This was more than an indiscretion; this could potentially have life altering consequences. The thought of an unwanted pregnancy sickened me.

I knew it would be the last time that Sam and I would be together, but what would happen if our indiscretion had consequences? I couldn't get over what had just happened once again; my ignorance and youth had allowed me to make a series of meaningful mistakes in my life. These events had complicated my existence, and now I was terrified that this sexual encounter might have consequences. I felt overwhelmed by the thought that I might be attached to Sam for the rest of my life. I was unhinged by an anger that evolved into hatred. The pity I had felt for him was gone. Nothing, not even a baby, could ever make me love him again.

Finally, after what felt like a lifetime of waiting, sharp cramps fully awakened me in the middle of a restless night to remind me of how lucky I was this time. I had never before felt so happy about a menstrual cycle. This pregnancy scare helped me realize that I had to end the charade with Sam. Sam was obsessed with me and I thought this had been his last desperate attempt to keep me in his life. I would be lying if I said I had the courage to tell him how I really felt. He was a beaten dog and I felt it unnecessary to be cruel. In the past I had tried to reason with him, "Sam, it is not right for either one of us to continue to stay together," but it had been in vain.

"Josefina, I want to marry you. I know we can be happy together, like in the beginning."

Frustrated, I sought out Sam's mother for support. She was a practical and broadminded woman, and I trusted that she would not judge me. I spoke to her with sincerity about the pregnancy scare. "I know it hurts him and I am sorry, but the problem is I am no longer in love with your son. Too much has happened between us."

She surprised me when she responded with kindness and understanding. "If you no longer love Sam, I support your decision to end the relationship." It was strange that she was the only adult I could turn to. I suppose she felt similar to me and did not want to prolong the inevitable. She agreed that too much had happened between us and that it was time to move on.

I knew what I wanted to do, but needed her to explain it to Sam. She agreed to meet with Sam and me. Together we explained that it had not been easy, but that I had made the decision to end the relationship. She said, "Sam, I am sorry but you have no choice but to accept it." She expressed compassion for us. She felt we had endured so many difficulties and she was sympathetic to both of us. To my surprise, he seemed to understand everything we were saying to him. I really appreciated her mediating on my behalf that day. She was able to make sense of it for Sam.

Sam's mother would never forgive my father for having provided the means to so many mistakes, but she was instrumental in helping me

learn the power of forgiving myself. Sam and my relationship was sour and doomed and she helped us both see it clearly.

In the past, Sam had made multiple efforts to continue his manipulation. He had claimed to suffer from separation anxiety, which frequently led to full-blown asthma episodes. He would threaten suicide if I abandoned him. He had pleaded we stay together because he loved me, he loved Gabriel, he loved my mother, and he even loved my father. He would make statements like, "Your family has been my family for years and I don't want to be without any of you." He finally understood that I could not continue with the lie. Sam knew it was over and he had no choice but to let me go.

Sam completed his house arrest and was carrying on under minimal supervision during his parole. He was free to start his life as a law-abiding citizen. After our relationship officially ended, I was inexplicably saddened by the break-up. I had grown so accustomed to his presence in my life, and felt nostalgic about the loss of innocence and the kids we were when we first met. I have since made peace with all the secrets I kept about our volatile relationship, and have forgiven him and myself for all of it.

Recently, I was pleased to hear that Sam became a successful business owner and is happily married. I no longer have resentment toward him and treasure the lessons we learned together. I have always wished him well and have been grateful that phase of my life ended, leaving me with the wisdom to make better choices in pursuit of my dreams. I recognize that along the way, through the pleasant and unpleasant experiences, I have gained appreciation for the powers that lie inside of me. With strength and certainty, I promised never again to allow myself to be manipulated into being someone I'm not.

CHAPTER 21

The attorney fees in Father's case were astronomical. Father instructed our mother to get a total of $40,000.00 out of a safe deposit box he kept at the bank. We had lived financially restricted lives. Mother was very thrifty and I really thought we always struggled monetarily. I was forced to get student loans to attend college, and Gabriel and I worked 40 hours a week while going to school full-time. We made our own car and insurance payments, and if we needed clothes or wanted personal items we would have to purchase it with our own money. It was a life of sacrifice and hard work for Gabriel and I; to find out our parents had a substantial amount of cash hidden away was irritating.

Mother explained, "I always suspected we needed to be ready for this possibility. If we didn't have any savings, your father would probably have to spend many years behind bars. None of us want that. Right?" As Gabriel and I listened to Mother's explanation, we understood the situation was dire and we all agreed that helping Father was a priority. We all loved him and wanted him to be home with us. We put our personal feelings aside about the hardships we had endured and agreed that it was a fortunate thing that we had the necessary means to hire a good attorney who could reduce the possibility of a long incarceration.

Father's top criminal defense attorney in Miami had sucked all the family's savings out of the bank and Mother had to cash out her retirement fund to make the last few installments. We were struggling to keep up with our financial obligations. Mother was piling up credit card debt related to the travel expenses required in order to meet the court's demands for appearances. We reduced some of the expenditures by agreeing to have only one person accompany Father to his court appearances. We took turns so that only two flight tickets instead of four would need to be purchased, and we always avoided hotel costs by staying at my cousin's house.

Perhaps it was due to my previous experience, or maybe my confidence in Father's defense attorney, but Father's case was not as traumatic as Sam's for me. I accompanied Father on the day the court was to make their final decision. The defense attorney had already made a plea bargain so we knew the outcome before we even stepped into court. The judge accepted Father's defense that he had acted in the capacity of interpreter, which made him an accessory to a crime rather than the main culprit. Thanks to the deal negotiated by the competent attorney and the prosecution's lack of additional evidence, Father was convicted of a low level offense. The court exercised mercy by accepting the prosecution's negotiations and dictating a lenient one-year and a half sentence of which he would spend ninety days in a federal prison.

It all felt very familiar. Similar to Sam, Father served his prison sentence and was transferred to serve thirty days in a half-way house, and later finished his sentence in house arrest where he was given permission to leave during the day for work while using an ankle bracelet as a monitoring device. Just like Sam, Father was allowed to slowly transition back into society. After the final phase of Father's sentence he was released with relatively minimum restrictions, required to report and stay under the supervision of a parole officer for the remainder of his sentence. Father paid his debt to society to its completion while I silently felt he deserved the consequences for his sins. It was the most contradictory emotion I had ever had concerning my father. I loved him, I hated him, I protected him, I attacked him, I was proud of him, and I was ashamed of him.

During his house arrest he began to look for work as part of the integration into society program. It had been almost fifteen years since he had last held a legitimate position. Prior to his getting involved in crooked business, he had worked for a large retail corporation but none of that mattered; he needed to start from scratch. The blemish on his record made things more difficult for him. As a convicted fifty-five year old felon, no one was knocking on his door with job offerings. Father was a natural salesman who became depressed and frustrated at the realization that his undeniable charisma was no longer enough. He had difficulty dealing with starting over at his age but he had no choice. Without any savings or real prospects, he found himself desperately in need of work, and accepted a job as an attendant at a local gas station. I felt his past shenanigans were so stupid. He took so many risks, shamed our family, put me in harm's way, and lived a disorganized existence, only to save up enough money to one-day become flat broke due to his financial obligation to attorney fees. Karma had completely caught up him. His most serious problem was that by this time Mother had become disappointed in him as a man. She went on to focus all her efforts on her career as an accountant, all the while becoming more and more distant from him. She allowed him to stay in the house because, as she put it, "He has nowhere else to go and he has no money." It hurt to see that she only felt sorry for him; after having adored him, he had finally and irreversibly fallen from grace in her eyes. In a twist, her pity for him awakened an unfamiliar, protective love from me to him. It was surreal to watch him weak and without options.

Conflicting feelings related to Father troubled me until November 27, 1989. An Avianca Boeing 727-100 flight 203 departing at 7:11 a.m. out of El Dorado International Airport in Bogota, Colombia, destination Alfonso Bonilla Aragon International Airport in Cali, exploded in mid-air only five minutes after its take off. Traveling at 493 mph at an altitude of 13,000 feet, the tragedy spared no survivors. The airplane was ripped apart, separating the nose section from the tail section. It descended in flames, killing all 107 people on board and three people on the ground, all victims of falling debris. Pablo Escobar, a well-known Colombian Drug Lord, had placed a bomb targeting Cesar Augusto Gaviria Trujillo, who had won the nomination for the Liberal Party candidacy and was campaigning for the Presidency. Gaviria was to be on this flight but had not boarded the plane due to security concerns. Among the victims who boarded the plane were three Americans citizens, which prompted the George H.W. Bush Administration to begin Intelligence Support Activity operations to catch Pablo Escobar.

My father was in the final phase of his sentence and at home the morning of the phone call. Tia Matilde, in a tearful voice said, "Octavio, they've killed Magdalena."

My father could barely let the words out of his mouth, "Who? What craziness are you saying to me? What are you saying?"

As if Tia Matilde did not hear Father's question, she continued, "She was always such a great girl. She never did anything bad to anyone. She was hardworking and a great mom to her two boys."

Father, very agitated, asked again, "Matilde, I'm listening to you but I don't understand."

Tia Matilde finally mustered the courage to utter the words. "She was on board that doomed flight this morning. She was on her way to a business meeting and now she's dead."

Father, shaken by the news he had just received, had to sit down. "Please, Matilde call the airline. Maybe she wasn't on the flight."

"NO! We already did. Her father has been on the phone all

morning. She was our only girl! How could this world be so cruel?" She desperately sobbed into the phone. Tia Matilde was inconsolable.

Father hung up the phone and for the first time I saw him cry like a baby. He said in a low voice, "Dios Mio! How could this be? I don't believe it!" He kept repeating it as if it was impossible for him to believe this had happened to such a great girl and such a kindhearted family. Magdalena had been studious, hard-working, always did the right thing, an outstanding young lady. How could this be? Tia Matilde was a compassionate woman who had dedicated herself to educating and helping children. Motherhood was her life's meaning and now all the sacrifices she had made with the dream of enjoying her beautiful daughter until the end of her time on earth was robbed in an instant. It was all too senseless to decipher, an agony too painful to accept.

Father was broken as he told us the horrible news. The grief I felt was indescribable. The horror played over in my mind, envisioning how she must have felt in those final moments was punishing. I prayed that she never saw it coming. I prayed that a simple switch was turned and, in a bright moment, she was in the presence of God. I prayed the pain was exclusively for those who loved her and lost her that day, not for her. My faith preached she was in peace but my mind had trapped memories of her kindness toward me, like a record player repeating the same song over and over. I knew she was a good soul and did not have to fear death, but there was that question I could not avoid. It kept creeping in my head. I wanted to silence my thoughts but I couldn't. In her final moments, I questioned if she was aware. Did she get a chance to send the people she loved her goodbyes? Did she get a chance to say a prayer?

Magdalena always treated me like a younger sister. She had shared her parents, her home, the stuffed teddy bear she kept on her bed, anything she owned, with me. I could still see her pretty smile and her beautiful, caramel eyes. She had consoled me throughout my parents' worst fights and now there was no way I could ever reciprocate.

After this senseless tragedy, it took me a long while to regain my trust in humanity. A deliberate act done by vicious, greedy animals had put an end to her shining life. There are no words to describe the moment when a person's optimism is completely gone. For me, it prompted questions about the world's purpose. I was frustrated to realize there were no answers that could raise my spirits. Magdalena's death gave me a new perspective on things that were blurry in the past. It defined the fact that there is an absolute right and a wrong. They are both separate things and should never be confused. The gray area is only possible because of ignorance. Now that gray area was gone.

Later that day, we watched the news and learned there were one hundred one passengers and six crewmembers aboard that flight. It was bizarre to hear that three people on the ground had been hit by the plane's debris and lost their lives that day. Many Colombian families, including ours, lost loved ones in the tragedy. I still could not comprehend how Tia Matilde lost her only daughter on this flight. Magdalena's tragic death was incredibly painful for a very long time. Our family and many Colombian families had participated directly or indirectly in creating a nation with terrible problems and we all had to pay a hefty price. Father made a statement that day I'll never forget, "Colombia is a nation enduring terrible losses due to the wrath of violent drug cartels. It is such a beautiful country with so much great natural wealth. There is gold, silver, iron, salt, platinum, emeralds, petroleum, coal, nickel, copper, wild orchids, coffee – no joda! – and so much more. Malparidos! All of it is now polluted by extremely evil parasites!"

As Father spoke, he had to make a great effort to hold back the tears.

My eyes were glassy as I heard his voice crack, words barely coming out of his mouth as he expressed sadness so deep. It was easy to see that at its core co-existed a heartfelt remorse. As a young girl who had experienced so many mixed feelings about my father, I, in that moment, witnessed a man face his demons and recognized he was ashamed. Tears ran down my face, as I understood he was a product of his surroundings. A surrounding that was now wrecking the lives of countless people. I made my peace with Father that tragic December day. He was ignorant to the reality that drug dealing was primarily for brutal criminals with superior ambitions than ours. He was not an evil man; I loved him, and I wanted to protect him. I went to him and hugged him tightly. I could smell the clean scent of the Jean Marie Farina cologne as I snuggled my head on his chest. Marks of running mascara on his white t-shirt was the only evidence that I was no longer a little girl.

While Father struggled to become a new man, he watched the news religiously. There seemed to be a new horror every day. He would say to Mother, "The citizens of Colombia are stuck in hell." I listened, but did not understand the entire conflict. For me, it was all too complicated. It was not easy for Colombian law-abiding citizens to unite efforts for stability and peace. Confronting the evils that plague the nation challenged people deeply due to the massive direct or indirect contribution to the problem. Father's observation was correct. It was hell. There were government officials of opposing political parties, paramilitary groups, rebels, drug cartels, etc. and every entity comprised of a group of people with self-serving interests. The insane part was that they all had contradicting agendas and all were willing to kill and die to achieve their purpose.

Colombia had lost sight of its many blessings and opted to engage in a battle against humanity. There was a general understanding of how difficult it would be to move forward. For many, a time of reckoning had come, and eventually only ruins for all who had refused to stop participating in the monstrosities.

CHAPTER 22

Overall, like Father, Colombia, through many adversities, got a grip during a time of crisis and began to repair what may have appeared to be irreparable mistakes. The time for pain slowly diminished, the time for healing was well on its way, and the time to strive for a better future had finally arrived.

As time passed, Father continued his efforts to overcome his grief while he dealt with the obstacles of having serious financial troubles. He worked a few jobs in a year's time. Mainly, he pumped gas at a fueling station. The bitter cold winter breeze circulated the area where the fuel dispensers sat, giving a wind tunnel-like effect where he stood and worked for eight hours a day. There was very little shelter from the elements and through it all, Father never complained. He was the most graceful I'd ever seen, and treated every customer special. If you didn't know any better you'd think he owned the place. He once asked me if one of my friends saw him working at the gas station, would I feel embarrassed.

Without hesitation I responded, "Embarrassed? Dad, no! Please never think that. I am glad that you have a job where you are safe." I did not want to hurt his feelings and did not have the courage to bring up the past. I knew the ugliness of his previous business and understood the consequences of it all. What I wanted to say was, "Dad, I am glad you are no longer involved in any sort of illicit dealings. Your past was embarrassing and shameful. This job at the gas station is respectable." I didn't complicate the answer with my true thoughts, I simply ended the conversation by giving him a hug.

Tio Cesar worked as the general manager of a midtown high rise. A position for a doorman became available and Tio Cesar was kind enough to offer Father the job. Father embraced the opportunity to earn a better wage and take advantage of the benefits of a steady income. I was glad he could finally get a break from the punishing winter cold and the excruciating summer heat. Tio Cesar knew Father's experience was mainly in sales and warned him there would be no room for growth in this position. Tio Cesar said, "Octavio, this is sort of a dead-end job, but don't worry, you are a people person so you'll enjoy it." Father was grateful and happy to take the position.

In a short time, he rediscovered the old work discipline he had acquired as a young boy. My grandfather had passed away when Father was only twelve years old. His older brothers went off to live their own lives while Father was left, forced to work long hours from a young age. He eventually withdrew from school for a full-time job to help support his sisters and his mother.

Lifting the heavy burden of ignominy from our family was where the doorman job held its true value. As he began to gain confidence, his charm began to resurface. His people skills kicked into high gear, making him a favorite and most loved doorman. All the tenants in the building appreciated and respected him. During Christmas he was showered with monetary gifts, and by the time he retired at seventy-five years of age, most of the tenants in the building pitched in to throw him a surprise retirement party. I attended the party and felt so much joy at the praises he received. Everyone had kind words about him, and could not say enough about how they thought he was a wonderful person. I heard many stories referencing his enthusiasm and unparalleled service. He had a willingness to help everyone with whatever their need was; luggage, kids, groceries, dogs, and sometimes just giving a big welcome home smile made people's day. I felt so much pride that night. He might as well have been retiring from a high ranked position. It was honorable to see how well he had redeemed himself. He had risen above the perils of ambition, selfishness, and arrogance. I knew for certain that was the real Octavio and that he was never going to change again. There were no more delusions of grandeur, no more shortcuts, no more cheap women, no more shame at this "dead-end job." Gabriel and I were very pleased but for Mother and Father, it was too late. She had closed her heart to him and nothing would ever change that.

As Father worked hard to reestablish peace in his life, my aunt and uncle in Colombia would never be able to recover from the loss of their daughter. My uncle became intolerant to those around him. He slowly lost his mind and eventually developed complete senility. He was ultimately put in a long-term care facility until he passed away. My loving aunt, a virtuous woman, could not bear the sorrow and died with only half her faculties, utterly grief stricken. These good people who had always worked hard to make the world a better place deserved more. For them, death would be their only rescue as they mourned the tragic loss of their daughter until their last days on earth.

I realized Father had been involved in criminal activities by default, and had personally suffered tragedies associated with the drug trafficking business. Apart from the disastrous loss of my beloved Magdalena, my other uncle, who was responsible for initiating Father into the business, the same man who owned a prosperous cattle ranch where I was able to drink warm milk straight out of one of his cows, lost his youngest daughter, Lucia.

I had spent time with Lucia during one of her visits to New York. She flew into Newark airport in New Jersey and Father was unable to pick her up so he asked me for the favor. I really didn't know Lucia well but I am now grateful that I was given the opportunity to do Father that favor. I still remember her radiant energy. She was slightly older than I, so she recognized me first when we made eye contact at the arrival terminal. She gave me a big smile and said, "Prima! Como estas? Tan linda!" We hugged one another tightly as if we knew each other well. She said, "Oh my goodness! You've turned out to be such a beautiful young lady. It's so wonderful to look at your face after all these years!"

Lucia kept a contagious, high-energy vibe. She had beautiful black hair and a light brown complexion. She was dressed very youthful and smelled like double mint gum and soft perfume. We walked to the parking lot with our arms interlocked. It was difficult for her to pull her luggage piece with just one hand so I asked her, "Do you need help? Want me to take your luggage?"

She responded, "No, its fine." She gave me a kiss on the cheek and politely let go of my arm. As soon as we got in the car she said, "Prima, I have this beautiful cassette. Play it so you can hear the music from your country."

I responded, "Of course, give it to me! I love Colombian music!" I put the cassette in the tape player and she turned up the volume.

"Prima! Listen to this vallenato, El Hambre del Liceo, it's about Santa Marta, where you were born. Rafael Escalona is a master!" It was hard for me to drive with so much noise, but I loved every minute of that moment in my life. She was carrying on and talking about my cousins back in Colombia and, for a brief moment, she noticed a woman driving a Mercedes Benz next to our car. She was looking at us snobbishly, and Lucia said, "What the heck! This lady thinks we are low class! Let's show her! She turned into the back seat of the car, opened her luggage and pulled out one of her underwear. She lowered the window and attached her underwear to the car's antenna and screamed out the window, "Ahi tienes vieja cara de verga!" I could not stop laughing. I had never experienced someone so vivacious and downright nuts. I laughed so much my stomach hurt. I could not believe this girl was so much fun. I nearly crashed from the outburst of laughter that came out of me. The lady in the Mercedes gave us a snooty look and decided to slow down and let us drive far ahead of her. From that moment on, we laughed constantly for almost the entire three days she spent at our house. Even when she was asleep she was funny. She snored like a grizzly bear and I found it amusing to see how her roar shook the walls in my bedroom.

She had friends in New York who invited her to a party. She asked me to come along and I agreed. I wanted to get my hair done so she accompanied me to the hair salon. The entire time we were there she kept coming up to me and asking, "Are you sure this is the style you asked for?" I was too embarrassed, and I couldn't look at the hairdresser or respond to the question. I knew she was right, my hair looked awful. The older woman doing my hair decided to do The Beehive on me. She teased and lacquered my hair until it was almost too big to walk out the door. It was so bad, and Lucia could hardly wait to poke fun at it. I walked out of the salon holding back the tears. As soon as the front door closed she put her arm around me and turned me toward the front of the salon. It had big, giant letters that said Coiffure. She looked at me and said, "Ahi Dios Mio! Coiffure! What the hell were you thinking? It's a party in New York and you chose a beehive hair style?"

We both bent over in front of the establishment and laughed until we were in tears. I said, "Lucia, I'm sure the hairdresser is looking at us right now. I feel so rude." She couldn't respond because she could barely catch her breath. At one point she pointed up at my head with one hand and with the other held her groin area because she felt her pee was coming out.

I really didn't feel upset at this point. It was so funny it almost made the bad hairstyle worthwhile. She said, "Hurry! I'm going to pee my pants!" She wiggled toward my car as I ran to open the car door. I sped off toward home in hopes no one would see me. All the while she joked, "Prima, I don't even think the right outfit could help you get away with it. The only power you can use to disguise that hair is shampoo and a good conditioner." She was tearing from all the high energy laughing and gasped in between words while trying to say, "That's the only thing I believe could help you in this moment."

I looked at her and a burst of laughter came out again. I was sorry she didn't live in the New York. I thought her and I could have been great friends. I loved her personality, especially the way she lightened up everything. She was one of the few people I've come across in life that could bring legitimate joy into a room. She was a colorful rainbow radiating brightness to all her surroundings. Her presence, her vibrant energy, was incredibly infectious and for many years it hurt to think about her tragic death. It was terrible that she had such a painful fate.

A few years after Lucia's visit to our house, she was kidnapped for ransom. My uncle was a wealthy man who was generally respected but Colombia was upside down and Lucia's only crime was that she was his daughter. Although the family adhered to all of the kidnapper's demands and made all efforts to rescue her, she was tortured and killed. Recordings of her pleading for mercy were mailed to her parents. It was a testimony that her captives were motivated by cruelty and evil. The many heinous acts committed by these low-life criminals clearly defined the difference between them and people like Father and his brother, who were merely looking for an easy score.

Facing criminal charges, the loss of Magdalena, and Lucia's unfortunate fate were not the only reasons Father closed the door on his past. He could not have conceived the dangers of Colombia's involvement in a destructive trade that victimized anyone they targeted without discrimination. The war was far from over but my dad no longer wanted to be a contributor. He understood all of it was warped, from the cocoa plantations in the remote jungle valleys, to clandestine labs, to ruthless distributors in the cities throughout the United States.

Many times I wondered how to make it all end. It was evident that nothing good could ever come of such dealings. Part of me understood we had to pay the price for our mistakes and accepted that moving forward was the only recourse left for all of us. I was grateful that the worst was behind us and looked forward to a new beginning.

Epilogue

I recently visited my Father and Mother. Shortly after I arrived, I fell asleep, exhausted from my trip. I thought I was dreaming when Father awakened me with his hand wrapped around a delicious chocolate milkshake. In that moment I saw his evolution clearly. With the milkshake in hand, I saw a younger man who could not distinguish right from wrong in his upbringing, who lived in a gray area of deception and betrayal to all he had promised loyalty to, but he loved me. Then I saw a mature man who struggled to put his life in order, who suffered the consequences of his mistakes, but he loved me. Finally, I saw a very thin, feeble, old man who still wants to work a part-time job to contribute to his house, who still treats me as if I was a little girl, and he loves me. And I love him. I love him as if he had never failed Mother, Gabriel, or me. He had earned it all back. Father is no longer the same selfish womanizer who was shamefully involved in illegitimate dealings, but he is the same wonderful dad. He worked in New York City in a genuine position with a respectful company for over 20 years, and even became a union member until his retirement.

Mother never divorced him. Instead, she passively handled her broken heart when she moved out of his bedroom twenty years ago. He never openly disrespected or abandoned her again. I've made peace with my dad. In that small apartment, without any luxuries, just my dad holding a chocolate milkshake in hand, I saw a man who had made terrible mistakes but whose heart had an immense ability for love, repentance, and redemption.

Although Mother's personality had two opposing traits, she was, is, and always will be my inspiration. I learned to value the two very distinct sides of her. Her most prevalent side was the one where she worked tirelessly, strived to rise above her limitations, stayed clean despite her dirty surroundings, and loved Gabriel and me above all things. The other side taught me the most difficult and valuable lessons; her willingness to put her own convictions aside due to the role she was expected to play as a woman in a "machista" male dominate world. Her weaknesses due to unrealistic insecurities allowed for the tampering of all she had worked to build.

All this helped shape my life for the better. The good and bad in her continues to be the foundation of my morals and ethics. I can't imagine what life would be like if she wasn't my mother. After all these years, Mother is completely disillusioned with her decision to accept Father back in her life. They live together but are no longer in love. She considers him a friend, a family member, but no longer is he the man that had the power to bring her happiness just by his mere presence. She no longer finds the old man attractive or interesting.

Father has endured years of reproach for a past that cannot be changed, and has accepted the kind of criticism that has become so common it ceased to have any effect or power. This too has been a lesson. In a quiet moment, Mother apologized for failing to establish a clear boundary for Father, and shared she had done what she believed was in our best interest. I responded by telling her that I respected and loved every effort she made to be a good parent and that I admired her as a woman. I don't want or need an apology from the person who has given so much to me. I love her with all her imperfections because, to me, she is the most perfect mother a girl could ever want.

Sam is in my past but I will forever remember the difficult lessons I learned with him. Today, I view it as a blessing that kick-started many good changes in all our lives. I am grateful that we, as a family, have regained balance, and I am glad that he managed to overcome his past and accomplished his goals legally.

I continued to work full-time while a student in a doctorate program, and am now a university Professor. I am no longer part of a gray area mindset that originated from a culture that was in terrible decay.

All the events that took place made me a resilient person. Today I am a proud mother who has taught her three children the evils of drug use, and the evils of hate. I will do all in my power not to allow their environment to dictate their future and their lives. I am teaching them to be decisive thinkers, to have a conscientious awareness of what is right and wrong and, through their decisions, dictate what their reality will be and determine what future they wish to pursue. I speak openly about the dangerous vulnerabilities that arise from ignorance and it is my sincere hope that one day they feel compelled to do the same for their children. For me, it has been a long journey, one that exposed me to dangers I was not prepared to face. I was fortunate to have a second chance. Although I was never convicted of a crime, like a prisoner I served a sentence of guilt, shame, and obligation to a loveless relationship that lasted almost five years.

I am a Professor in the Department of Ethnic Studies at a prestigious university. My doctorate degree did not come easy. I faced considerable odds, starting with having to overcome ideas about who I was so that I could move forward. Every achievement I've ever accomplished has served as a reminder of how far my family and I have come in the transformation from new immigrants to established citizens of the United States of America. I've learned valuable lessons that have helped me move forward and inspired me to follow my dreams. I don't judge my Mother. I love her, and I admire her. I understand she was taught to specifically follow roles that had been predetermined by patriarchal societies. I can only imagine how difficult it must have been for her to put her own happiness aside for the sake of what she believed would bring my brother and me the most stability, and I continue to admire her courage.

Gabriel is still my best friend. Throughout different periods in our lives we found comfort in being each other's playmate, confidant, therapist, and all the other things that family can be for one another. The confusion is over for Gabriel. He also found our upbringing difficult but not impossible to overcome. He and I spooked one another when we shared a dream about a man in a white robe that roamed our house in Colombia. We were both scared to death of the common experience but also felt fortunate about how in synch we always seemed to be. He and I are soul mates in friendship and nothing will ever get in the way of our relationship. I am proud to say that Gabriel was inspired to be different. He is a terrific family man who loves his children above all things. Although we are all grown up, we still get together and goof around as if we were kids. He has been a blessing in my life and I feel very fortunate to be his sister.

I am happy that Colombia is no longer the cocaine capital of the world and hopeful that one day it will make the necessary social reforms to offer its people prosperity. In my dreams Colombia's malevolence will seize and it will use all the blessings of a well-endowed country to one day boom. For now, I am happy that it is no longer a country that believed it could pray to God while engaging in acts against humanity. My hope is that it continues the struggle to rectify its extreme violence and the remnants of the drug epidemic.

I give thanks to my parents every day for offering Gabriel and me a life in this blessed land. I feel fortunate to have had the experiences which fueled my determination to live my life with honesty, far from all that represents my past.

My name is Josefina Lopez, and my story continues.

History As I Understand It

The bombing of the Avianca flight was one of many terrorizing measures used by the Medellin drug cartel in their sustained struggles to maintain free reign to conduct their illicit business. In the 1970s and 1980s, Colombia was credited for being one of the main suppliers of illegal cocaine and marijuana smuggled into the United States. The United States and Colombian governments aligned forces in an effort to battle the drug epidemic. As a result of the collaborative efforts, the two countries signed what was intended to be a model antinarcotics program, the bilateral Extradition Treaty, in 1979. In negotiating the terms of the treaty, Colombia agreed to extradite captured drug dealers to the United States in exchange for $26 million dollars in assistance via training and equipment for the purpose of fighting the drug trafficking problem.

In response to the alignment between the two governments, drug traffickers, along with rebel groups, engaged in a series of systematic assaults through extortion, kidnapping, trafficking of drugs, trafficking of arms, political assassinations, and bombings. They targeted the very core of Colombia as they commenced multiple attacks on government buildings. Among the most infamous was the siege of The Palace of Justice on November 6, 1985 by the Colombian guerrilla known as the M19, or the April 19 movement. Twenty-five Supreme Court Justices and hundreds of other civilians were held hostage as the M19 demanded the justices convict Colombian President Belisario Betancur and Defense Minister Rodrigo Lara Bonilla for violating a supposed peace agreement they had made with the rebel group a year and a half earlier. The M19 was primarily referring to President Betancur's changing his previous nationalistic rhetoric where he favored a nonaligned position and solidarity between Latin America and the Third World. He had opposed the Reagan administration because he disagreed with their intervention in Central America and was critical of the United States' attempts to isolate Cuba and Nicaragua.

In the beginning of Betancur's term, he had embraced patriotic trade policies. He refused to increase his contribution to the International Monetary Fund (IMF) and the Inter-American Development Bank (IDB). He also fell short to his commitment to target and reduce the drug trafficking problem as North Americans demand for drugs continued to increase. However, in 1985, Betancur changed his position on drug related issues. He understood that his refusal to contribute to the IMF and IDB had placed the government in a financial crisis. More importantly, he had a new awareness of the narcotic-related corruption in politics, as well as the drug abuse among Colombian youth. He had initially refused to extradite any Colombian Nationals to the United States as a matter of principle, but shifted and began to implement severe measures against the cartels while he worked in cooperation with the United States' antidrug trafficking campaign. In exchange for his new approach, the U.S. provided support during Colombia's debt negotiations with the IMF and the World Bank. Betancur's new and more pragmatic foreign relations stance angered many rebels and cartel members.

During the siege, many people in the Palace of Justice were murdered, others disappeared and were never accounted for. Ultimately, the building was set on fire and documents for an estimated six thousand criminal cases were destroyed, severely damaging the legal system and officially ending President Betancur's efforts to reach peace between the M19 paramilitary group and another rebel group known as the Revolutionary Armed Forces of Colombia (Fuerzas Armadas Revolucionarias de Colombia), referred to as the FARC.

The FARC came to exist in the late 1960s and had fought for the equality of citizens through communism; however, they shifted their agenda in the mid-1980s. The FARC violated its own original purpose, as it partook in immeasurable human rights violations while in the business of drug trafficking and terrorism.

Despite fearful circumstances, political figures and officials in Colombia battled on. One of the most notable public servants to declare war against the drug cartels was Rodrigo Lara Bonilla. As Minister of Justice under President Betancur, Rodrigo Lara dedicated all his efforts through the use of intelligent forces to detect illegal activities. Lara was a brave man who dared to expose the infiltration of drug money into Colombia's politics. He confronted and uncovered Pablo Escobar, one of the known ringleaders who, at the time, was a deputy member of the Colombian congress, as a leading drug lord and demanded he be boot out of congress. He also invalidated Escobar's visa to the United States and began a crusade to eliminate his dealings and that of the Medellin Cartel. Rodrigo Lara took part in many heroic acts. He worked tirelessly alongside a brilliant officer of the National Police, Colonel Jaime Ramirez Gomez. Together they planned, organized, located, and exposed a massive operations base for cocaine production. The complex was known as Tranquilandia (Tranquility Land), as it was hidden deep within the jungles of Colombia, located in the southern Department of Caqueta. The complex lab had the capacity to utilize chemicals such as acetone, benzene, ethyl ether, hydrochloric acid, sodium carbonate, sodium sulfate, sulfuric, and so on, to refine 23.733 kilos of cocaine in a short six months. It was an astounding arrangement comprised of nineteen sophisticated labs and eight clandestine runways for jumbo airplanes to safely land. It had comfortable living quarters, which was supplied with water from the nearby Yari River, and electricity through the use of powerful generators. It was estimated that more than two thousand people lived and worked there, making and packaging cocaine at the Tranquilandia. Rodrigo Lara and Colonel Ramirez Gomez, together with the assistance of the DEA, targeted Tranquilandia and the biggest names in the Medellin Cartel; Jose Gonzalo Rodriguez Gacha, Jorge Luis Ochoa Vasques, Juan David Ochoa Vasques and Fabio Ochoa Vasques, Pablo Escobar, and Carlos Lehder.

The cartel made a particularly detrimental mistake when it purchased 76 barrels of ether from Chicago, Illinois and imported it to the Tranquilandia facility. The barrels had been tagged by the DEA, unequivocally divulging the complex's location. On March 10th, 1984, the information was used to raid and ultimately completely destroy the facility.

The lab's exposure, the successful raid, the destruction of the compound, Lara's successful seizure of the properties of as many as thirty drug lords via 150 small planes and helicopters used for drug trafficking, as well as his executive order to deny operational licenses to airlines that were suspected of corruption, sealed a death sentence for both Rodrigo Lara Bonilla and Colonel Ramirez Gomez.

Our family, along with many other Colombian families, lamented when the anti-drug Justice Minister Rodrigo Lara Bonilla was assassinated on April 30, 1984 by two men on red Yamaha motorcycles who pulled up alongside his car and shot him seven times. He died in the presence of his eight-year-old son. It was not just retribution, he was killed as a means to eliminate his efforts to continue to prosecute cocaine traffickers in the Medellin Cartel. Lara's death led to Escobar's indictment for murder and prompted President Betancur to immediately launch a "war without quarter" against the cartel. The Colombian government's decision to extradite drug traffickers to the United States marked the start of a war against organized crime and one of the darkest eras in Colombia's history. From November 1984 to June 1987, thirteen nationals were extradited, including Drug Lord Carlos Lehder Rivas, who was convicted in May 1988 of massive drug trafficking and remains in a maximum-security prison to this day.

Colonel Ramirez was an ethical man who had worked alongside Lara and had fearlessly accused Pablo Escobar of being the mastermind behind Minister Lara's death. The Colonel retired from the police narcotics unit and was awaiting ascension to General when he was assassinated while traveling with his wife on November 17, 1986. He would not be the last targeted official or high profile citizen to fall victim to the crime spree.

Among the esteemed citizens I believe should be honored as fallen heroes is the editor of the newspaper, El Espectador, who considered himself a defender of freedom of the press. Guillermo Cano Isaza was assassinated on December 17, 1986 in retaliation for a movement he had launched using the newspaper to publicly denounce and expose the influence of drug traffickers in the country's politics.

Despite all the measures taken by President Betancur during his presidency, in June 1987, under the new administration of President Virgilio Barco Vargas, the Colombian Supreme Court declared the United States/Colombian extradition treaty unconstitutional and annulled it. The annulment of the treaty was not only a setback to the antidrug efforts but it tied the hands of the authorities in the United States who had many extradition cases pending, most significantly against Pablo Escobar, Jose Gonzalo Rodriguez Gacha and one of the Ochoa brothers, Jorge Luis, who were main leaders of the Medellin Cartel. During that time, the Colombian Congress was hesitant to resubmit the extradition legislation because some of its members had been threatened and were fearful, and others had received bribes and were corrupt.

The United States protested after the Ochoa brothers were released from prison on December 1987. Reports estimated that 80 percent of the cocaine consumed in the streets of America was imported from Colombia by the Medellin Cartel and its rival, the Cali Cartel. Despite the United States' alarmed position, on May 1988 the Colombian Supreme Court rejected the use of existing laws to extradite more Colombian drug traffickers to the United States for trial.

Washington D.C., under the George H.W. Bush administration, was under pressure to battle against the increasing drug usage and drug related violence in many cities throughout the U.S. Once again, they set forth a proposal for Colombian officials to enforce the extradition law. It was thought of as a good way to solve the epidemic of drug addiction in the U.S., and lower crimes related to drug trafficking in Colombia. The rational was that incarcerating the heads of the trafficking industry in a legitimate, uncorrupted United States prison would obstruct the continuation of their operations by restricting drugs suppliers from doing any business behind bars. Colombia's contemplation of the proposal and the process leading up to enforcing the extradition agreement with the United States ignited a war that would claim thousands of lives. It was the drug traffickers' response to the only fear they had; serving a sentence in a U.S. prison. They continued to terrorize Colombian citizens and government officials by accomplishing several high profile assassinations.

The violence continued after the bombing of the Avianca flight 203. A week later on the morning of December 6, 1989, United States Attorney, General Dick Thornburgh, announced that authorities had frozen accounts in five countries holding $61.8 million belonging to the notorious drug lord, Rodriguez Gacha. In response, on the very same day, the Administrative Department of Security, also known as the DAS, headquartered in Bogota, Colombia, was bombed. Sixty-three people were killed and over a thousand were injured. An indication that violence was prevailing, its purpose was to send a clear, intimidating message to government officials who struggled to stand on the side of justice. The criminals, its followers and its rivals, all involved, were fearless and defiant to the law. There were countless stories of massacring of judicial officials, politicians, law enforcement officers, and wealthy citizens, as well as merciless kidnappings of children, and anyone whom the delinquents felt compelled to target. Nothing was sacred. The reign of terror continued as several assassinations of presidential hopefuls occurred, leaving the people of Colombia in a state of disarray. They not only attacked Colombia's legal system, but also demonstrated no respect for life, transforming Colombia into the murder capital of the world by 1991.

I read about the politics of the country because I wanted to make sense of my cousin Magdalena and Lucia's deaths. It was hard to believe how many notable people had become the cartel victims.

Among the long list was Luis Carlos Galan, a candidate for the presidency of Colombia, representing the Liberal Party. He had declared himself an enemy of the dangerous drug cartels, specifically the Medellin Cartel and its ruthless leaders, Rodriguez Gacha and Pablo Escobar. He received several death threats before his assassination on August 18, 1989. He died while working a public demonstration in the town of Soacha, Cundinamarca at the hands of the same faction responsible for much of the terrorist acts at the time.

Evil has never existed by itself; good resurfaced in the acts of other brave men like Cesar Augusto Gaviria who picked up the torch after Luis Carlos Galan's assassination and battled to keep the delicate balance. He, too, opposed the corruption of the Colombian society at all levels and supported the extradition treaty with the United States. He became the target in what I considered the most significant of the terrorist acts, the bombing of the Avianca flight where my beloved Magdalena perished. The attack was a failed mission since it did not kill the intended target, Cesar Augusto Gaviria; instead it elevated the animosity held against the cartels. Our family and many others held them responsible for the deaths of thousands of well-intended as well as ill-intended Colombians. Many grieved, as the country was further divided. It was a bloody war between the profit earners and the people who longed for stability and peace. Galan was killed after he publicly declared he would align efforts with the United States. He believed it would be the only effective deterrent against criminals who had enjoyed a free reign. His courageousness earned him a fallen hero's medal in the history books, as he became another political candidate brutally assassinated without accomplishing a resolve to the problem of widespread delinquency.

It seemed like all was not in vain. In the midst of all the chaos and unrest laid an inspired and motivated community with the determination to honor and continue with Galan's quest. Galan's death catapulted a police movement to hunt down billionaire leader of the Medellin cartel, Jose Gonzalo Rodriguez Gacha. He had been indicted in the United States and was accused of forcing President Virgilio Barco Vargas of abandoning his anti-drug war, as well as assassinating Galan. Police efforts paid off on December 16, 1989, when they gunned down Gacha in a rural area near Covenas and Tolu, south of Cartagena.

The civil war, fueled by Colombia's cocaine trade, destabilized every facet of society. Other political murders followed and most political figures were in danger despite security efforts. Whether it was a public servant from a legitimate political family or a rebel turned to politics, there was no safe haven for anyone aspiring to lawfully or unlawfully succeed in attaining a political position. Case in point was presidential hopeful, Bernardo Jaramillo Ossa. A former terrorist himself, he transformed into the leader of the newly formed Patriotic Union Party, and was assassinated on March 22, 1990. Jaramillo Ossa was supposedly under the protection of the Administrative Department of Security DAS–(Departamento Administrativo de Seguiridad) but was shot to death while his wife accompanied him when he was campaigning in Bogota. His past associations with rebel groups did not shield him. He had somehow become an enemy of the corruption that ran rampant. There were suspicions that a member of the DAS worked in cahoots with the assailants.

Ossa sought politics originally in the Colombian Communist Party. He was a Marxist who gained a seat of Senator of the Republic, a socialist international who wanted to end any suspicions of his affiliation with the rebel group La FARC. He was a candidate for the Presidency and planned to join alliance with Carlos Pizarro Leongomez who was also a former terrorist leader of the guerilla group, the 19th of April Movement (M-19), which later officially converted to a new political party known as the M-19 Democratic Alliance. Leongomez also became part of the list of Presidential candidates assassinated. Leongomez was killed on April 26, 1990, and replaced by Antonio Navarro Wolff. Wolff would not hold the position long since hundreds of members of the Patriotic Union party were assassinated, resulting in the party's withdrawal from the elections.

After the ferocious election, on May 27, 1990, Cesar Augusto Gaviria Trujillo of the Liberal Party, the only target of the fatal Avianca flight 203, won the election. As President, he summoned the Constituent Assembly of Colombia and enacted the Constitution of 1991. Gaviria was born into a prominent family recognized as principal figures in the economy and politics of the country. He was the debate chief for Luis Carlos Galan during his 1989 presidential campaign. He had not only become Galan's political successor after Galan's assassination, but also Pablo Escobar's target. He joined forces with the United States, leading the fight against the Medellin drug cartel, Cali drug cartel, and various guerrilla factions who had created paramilitary groups funded by traffickers to protect the coca fields, the labs, and the smuggling routes. He signed an extradition agreement with the United States which sent a strong message of hope to the people of Colombia, and one of noncooperation to the drug lords who only feared the American prisons.

Hundreds of officials, journalists, attorneys, businessmen, and innocent bystanders had fallen victim to the extreme darkness that had plagued Colombia, but a bit of hope finally emerged. Citizens regained some confidence that things would begin to change. Thanks to the fearless Colombian officials who refused to cave in to the demands of the drug cartels and the paramilitary groups, there were finally signs that wicked forces were weakened.

The extradition legislation had been significant as it was the only indisputable deterrent drug traffickers feared and resented. They felt only Colombia had the jurisdiction to imprison its citizens for crimes committed on their soil. Escobar continued to successfully manipulate Colombia's legal system. After his conviction, he served his prison sentence in a jail he built. It was a luxurious facility, a prison called The Cathedral (La Catedral). Its purpose was to house himself while he served time. The corrupted prison enabled Escobar to continue controlling his drug empire and proceed with arranging the murders of his rivals. Escobar and all his thugs were aware that they could not fraudulently serve time in an American prison or manipulate the United States justice system. He escaped La Catedral on July 20, 1992 after he was informed that he was being transferred out of La Catedral.

The Colombian people were fed up with the chaos that had afflicted an otherwise beautiful land. There were many people who mustered up the courage to stand for the ideal to bring Colombia back to a place where safety and prosperity for its citizens superseded an evil ambition. These were patriotic times and people willingly paid with their lives to end the insanity. On December 2, 1993, under the Gaviria administration, Colombian police gunned down one of its biggest menaces, Pablo Escobar, earning Gaviria a significant triumph that sent a message of hope for all those who opposed the narcotrafficking business. With the aid of American advisors and equipment, the Colombian army was finally able to rid the country of the rebel, the decision maker in a so-called group known as The Extraditable (Los Extraditables) whose motto was: "We prefer a grave in Colombia to a prison in the United States." Escobar was finally killed in Medellin.

Three Ochoa brothers pled guilty to certain crimes in the 1990s and plea-bargained with the Colombian government. After they won the extradition battle, they went on to serve a five-year sentence in Colombia. All three brothers were released in 1996. The Ochoa brothers were from a wealthy family in the restaurant, raising horses, and cattle breeding businesses. Juan David Ochoa Vasquez, the oldest of the Ochoa brothers, had a ranch he owned in Central Florida where 39 Paso Fino horses were seized by the U.S. government in 1987. After he served his prison time he returned to his family's business and went on to legally raise horses. He expressed his family's regret for having been involved in the trafficking business and died of a heart attack in a medical clinic in Medellin at the age of 65.

Jorge Luis Ochoa Vasquez was the second brother. He claimed a friend involved him in the business and, because he had no life experience, he became wrapped into a situation that snowballed. He stated the demand for drugs was so high that the business thrived without much effort. In the end, it brought his family more trouble than the money was worth. He credited Escobar for being the only reason there was any viciousness. He shed all personal responsibility for having been involved in responding to the fear of extradition with violence. He was of the opinion that the United States would have a better handle on the problem if it legalized, controlled the distribution of drugs, and educated its youth. Failure to do this would mean that the problem would remain a continual battle. He thought controlling people or preventing them from using drugs was a difficult task. He regrets his involvement in the business and asked for forgiveness. He now pleads on behalf of his youngest brother, Fabio Ochoa Vasquez, who was extradited to the U.S. in 2003. He was convicted on two counts of drug conspiracy and is currently serving a thirty-year sentence in a U.S. federal prison after having served five years in a Colombian prison for unrelated charges. He believes his brother is being treated unfairly and that the law should not be vengeful. He stated that his parents, sisters, and whole family never approved of the brothers' involvement in the business. They remain a sad but close-knit family.

Carlos Enrique Lehder Rivas created a route to smuggle drugs from a private Island called Norman's Cay in the Bahamas into the United States. He was one of the first leaders of the cartel to be extradited and convicted of drug trafficking in 1987. He was given a life sentence without the possibility of parole plus 135 years in a United States federal prison. In an effort to reduce his sentence, he entered a cooperation agreement with the U.S. in 1991. He agreed to testify against General Manuel Noriega of Panama and in exchange was promised a reduced sentence of 30 years. After he gave testimony, he was placed in the witness protection program as an incarcerated witness but his sentence was only reduced to 55 years. In 2015 he wrote a letter to Colombian President Juan Manuel Santos where he pleads for the President to intervene with the U.S. authorities. In the letter, Ledher stated after twenty-eight years in captivity and now close to 67 years of age, he believes he deserves to die in Colombia.

Gacha, Escobar, Lehder, and the Ochoa brothers originated and organized a billion-dollar drug smuggling business. For their contributions they earned death and prison sentences. In Colombia the struggle for justice continues but some good had triumphed over evil, finally replacing violence with some hope. Decades later, former President Gaviria continues to do work for non-profit organizations, and still promotes democracy and change in the international community. Although an unknown gunman gunned down his sister, Lilliana Gaviria in 2006, he has never wavered in his contribution to the stabilization of Colombian politics.

Regrettably, addiction traveled like a poison, steadily through a direct path to the North American continent, a path that impacted millions of Americans with great force. Escobar's death allowed the Cali cartel to capitalize on the Medellin cartel's weakness, and for years there would be a bloody rivalry between the two cartels. The Medellin cartel created chaos in Colombia while the Cali cartel operated cells in several states including Florida, Texas, Arizona and California, with each cell reportedly distributing a staggering $500,000.00 a day. The traffickers were organized in studying the legal system in the U.S. They understood how lawyers, prosecutors and DEA agents operated. Typically, after traffickers were caught, they would post bail and skip town. Very rarely did they await prosecution. They diligently studied the methods of the U.S. government's legal system in the hopes of staying one step ahead of the law.

The war continued, and between the years 2000 and 2010, a little over one thousand drug traffickers had been extradited to the United States. Additionally, the Citizen Security Law was enacted on June 24, 2011. It analyzed the complexity of the problem and acknowledged that provisions of the extradition laws alone were not the solution. The effectiveness of extradition had become questionable because it granted criminals some leverage. The United States judicial system, in consideration of the time sensitive factors in a case and the value of the informants' contribution, offered captured drug dealers legal benefits in exchange for information. For instance, some negotiated prison term reductions, protection for themselves and their families, and the ability to secure part of their wealth. Another favorable benefit was the option to expedited extradition. In the past, captive drug traffickers had to spend two years in a Colombian prison while the courts reviewed the United States' extradition request. The new law simplified and expedited the extradition process by giving the arrested criminal the right to waive his appeal for extradition and the Colombian courts twenty days to decide whether or not he or she would be extradited. In the past, the two year criminals sat in a Colombian jail and any time served was not discounted in the United States penal system, making expediting the extradition a better option since they would be better off counting any time served toward their sentencing in a U.S. prison.

Some still view extradition as a controversial law for the sovereignty of Colombia and an ineffective burden on the U.S. judicial system. I believe there was a time when it did effectively interrupt drug traffickers' momentum. Colombia did benefit from using extradition as a weapon to block some of the criminal activities. During the peak of Colombia's global reign on the drug market, there was very little alternative. Colombia's legal system had fallen prey to the overwhelming delinquency of the various entities; cartels, paramilitary groups, corrupted officials, and others conducting illegal business openly or with little legal consequences.

There may not be one answer to the entire complicated problem, but most solutions are flawed. I am uncertain if reform could exist solely through an aligned collaborative effort between the U.S. and Colombia. True change must also consider ways to strengthen the Colombian government's ability to fight against the various entities involved in organized crime. They need to consider the various factors at the root of the problem. A true transformation is impossible unless the Colombian government initiates social restructuring. I clearly remember walking a main avenue in Bogota when, in plain daylight, a couple of "Gamines", young homeless boys not more than twelve to fourteen years of age, violently pulled Mother's hair. Her neck shifted backward as one of them swiftly put his filthy hands on her face and pulled her gold chain off. As a young girl I obsessed over that awful incident for a long time. As an adult, I refer back to the experience and it prompts me to connect criminal activity to extreme poverty.

The widespread poverty, economic instability, and desperation of the people gave little options to those youngsters starving in the streets. The Colombian government needs to offer its citizens who are disadvantaged an opportunity to have safety and better economic opportunities. Education and job opportunities with respectable wages may be perceived as a better option to crime. It would also rob the appeal away from taking part in criminal activity. Social reform may involve new and more reasonable legislation that not only considers drug trafficking when rendering a sentence, but legal entities also need to acknowledge the crimes committed against humanity before deciding consequences. They cannot continue to ignore the real social problems if they truly want to the restoration of civic order.

The use of cocaine created addiction, prostitution, and complete disorder in certain American cities, which forced a war against drugs in the United States as it did in Colombia. Today, the United States relies much less on informants to solve cases. They manage to stay on top of the game through the use of technology and intelligence gathering. They've adopted a more competent system where authorities follow the money instead of the drugs.

I love the United States with all my might. My children were born in America and I hope to die in America. Sadly, the U.S. continues to struggle with the highest drug consumption in the world. The war on drugs will probably never cease. Educating youngsters to "Just Say No" is a good start, but the U.S. needs to consider laws that shift a distributors' ability to make financial gain. For now, I am morally relieved that Colombia's contribution in the marketplace has been reduced significantly. I am confident that America will continue its efforts to keep its citizens, particularly its children, off drugs. I am optimistic that this great country will not fall to the same inequalities and injustices evident in other countries throughout the world.

About the Authors

Ingrid O. Duva and Betty O. McAleer are the coauthors of White Powder Fences. Their realistic fictional story resonates with a large community of culturally diverse immigrants who battle to adjust not only to a new geographical location but also to a set of social rules that may differ and at times conflict with his or her upbringing and mindset. In this coming of age story the authors pay tribute to two cultures through the experiences of the protagonist, Josefina.

Ingrid O. Duva is also an expert English-Spanish translator and interpreter. You can find her on Facebook and Twitter.

Betty O. McAleer is also a lover of history, a wife, and a mother of two. You can find her on Facebook and Twitter.

92106226R00130

Made in the USA
Middletown, DE
05 October 2018